'Twelve superheroes *and* the secrets of Superman's private* life revealed . . . If this book doesn't get you putting on a mask and secret underwear and swinging out the nearest window to do battle with the forces of evil – then there's no hope for you . . .'

From the Introduction to SUPERHEROES

* Publisher's commercial footnote: for 'private' read 'sex'

Superheroes

Edited by MICHEL PARRY

SPHERE BOOKS LIMITED
30/32 Gray's Inn Road, London WC1X 8JL

First published by Sphere Books Ltd 1978

To Jerry Siegel and Joe Shuster, who started it all –
and to Stan Lee, for keeping the Torch alight.

TRADE
MARK

Set in VIP Baskerville on the Pentamatic System

Printed in Great Britain by
Hazell Watson & Viney Ltd
Aylesbury, Bucks

Acknowledgements

Stuporman by Robert Bloch, copyright 1943 by the Ziff-Davis Publishing Company for Fantastic Adventures, June, 1943. Reprinted by permission of the author's agents, A. M. Heath Ltd and the Scott Meredith Literary Agency.

The Evil Super-Man by George E. Clark, copyright 1940 by the Western Fiction Publishing Company, Inc for *Marvel Tales*, May, 1940. Originally published as *The Test-tube Monster*.

The Golden Amazon Returns by John Russell Fearn, copyright 1940 by the Ziff-Davis Publishing Company for Fantastic Adventures, 1940. Reprinted by permission of Mrs Carrie Fearn and the Cosmos Literary Agency.

Origin of a Superhero by Donald F. Glut, © 1978 by the author. Original to this collection.

Captain Amazing by Stephen Hitchcock, © 1978 by the author. Original to this collection.

The Awesome Menace of 'The Polarizer' by George Alec Effinger, © 1971 by the Ultimate Publishing Co. Inc. Published by arrangement with the author.

Satyr-Man by John A. Keel, © 1966 by Fawcett Publications, Inc for THE FICKLE FINGER OF FATE. Reprinted by permission of the author's agent, Mr Knox Burger, 39½ Washington Square South, N.Y. 10012.

Transmuto, the Metamorphic Myrmidon by Adrian Cole, © 1978 by the author. Original to this collection.

Easy Way Out by Marion Pitman, © 1978 by the author. Original to this collection.

It's a Bird, It's a Plane! by Norman Spinrad, © 1967 by the Dugent Publishing Company for *Gent*. Reprinted by permission of the author's agents, A. M. Heath Ltd and the Scott Meredith Literary Agency.

Up, Up and Away by Allan C. Kimball, © 1978 by the author. Original to this collection.

Alternative Ending by Frank Adey, © 1978 by the author. Original to this collection.

Man of Steel, Woman of Kleenex by Larry Niven, © 1971 by the author. Reprinted from ALL THE MYRIAD WAYS by permission of the author's agent, Leslie Flood.

Thanks are also due to Karl Edward Wagner for his suggestions and advice.

Contents

Introduction

'Look . . . up in the sky . . . it's a bird . . . it's a plane . . . it's SUPERMAN!'

Superman TV series

'Beware of the man whose god is in the skies.'

George Bernard Shaw, *Man and Superman*.

In the beginning was the bird – and the bird, of course, was Superman.

The familiar figure in the red and blue flying suit seems to have been with us for as long as most of us can remember. In fact, the Man of Steel leapt his first tall building in the late thirties, the brainchild of two teenage Science Fiction fans from Cleveland, Ohio. Jerry Siegel wrote the captions and dialogue and his close friend Joe Shuster drew the pictures. When Siegel first dreamt up the idea of the super-strong refugee from the planet Krypton, they were both just seventeen.

Success didn't come easily. Just as record companies later gave the unknown Beatles the brush-off, so comic-strip publishers rejected *Superman* as too fanciful, too uncommercial . . . It took Siegel and Shuster five years to find a buyer for the first strip. The world's best-known illegal immigrant finally made his debut in the June 1938 issue of *Action Comics*. Reader response was encouraging. By the following year, Superman had graduated to a comic-book of his own, heralded as the 'World's Greatest Adventure Strip!' Within two years, millions were following his exploits on the radio. Films and a long-running TV series followed. By then Superman had become a household name; he joined Sherlock Holmes and Dracula and Frankenstein in the ranks of the Immortals.

Superman's success opened the floodgates: a deluge ensued. Suddenly, every publisher in the comic-book business (and there were more of them in those days) wanted a Superman of his own, preferably a dozen. Before Superman there had been only heroes. After Superman came hordes of *super*heroes, brightly-coloured legions of them (so many it's surprising there weren't more mid-air collisions!) Some were more super than others and some, it has to be said, were not really very super at all.

One of the pitfalls facing early publishers intent on capitalizing on Superman's success was – how did *their* superheroes come to have acquired their super-attributes in the first place? Obviously they couldn't all have made the same one-way trip from Krypton or accusations of plagiarism (accompanied, no doubt, by expensive lawsuits) would swiftly follow. As Jules Feiffer points out in *The Great Comic Book Heroes*, writers delegated to solve the problem sought for solutions among the Marvels of Modern Science (i.e. *comic-book* Science): 'That strange bubbly world of test-tubes and gobbledy-gook which had, in the past, done such great work in bringing the dead back to life in the form of monsters – why couldn't it also make men super?'

It could, of course – and presently began to do so with alarming and ever-increasing regularity. (As some of the stories in the present collection will show, a good dependable rule in comics and pulp SF has always been: *When in doubt, send for a mad scientist!*) Steve Rogers, the kind of nebbish accustomed to having to claw sand out of his eyes at the beach, entered the laboratory of a certain Professor Reinstein – and came out strapping, dynamic, star-spangled Captain America! Many more followed a similar path, emerging from labs all over the U.S. with sideboard shoulders, a steely gaze and a new purpose in life. Tailors who could be trusted to keep their mouths shut made a fortune running up costumes in styles and colours previously undreamt of outside of Frederick's of Hollywood.

No strange elixirs, painful injections or unorthodox surgery were necessary for young Billy Batson to become a superhero. All he had to do was utter the magic (and acrostic) word *SHAZAM!* for the cumulative, polytheistic qualities of Solomon-Hercules-Atlas-Zeus-Achilles and Mercury to be miraculously bestowed on him, instantly transforming him from a slender button-eyed teenager into a mature, muscular figure in vivid red leotard and white comic opera cape – the World's Mightiest Mortal, Captain Marvel. Unfortunately, along with the rest of his marvellous qualities, the Captain also inherited an Achilles heel – which, in his case, turned out to be a not unnoticeable similarity to Superman. The Superman publishers sued the Captain Marvel publishers for plagiarism. The Captain's side lost and the 'Big Red Cheese' (as he was labelled by his less kindly adversaries) was packed off into the long, enforced exile from which he has only recently made a welcome return.

In the stampede to copy Superman's super-success, many were called but few arrived, the obvious losers soon dropping back into the mists of obscurity: instant trivia-quiz questions. Other heroes, either more imaginative or just plain lucky, managed to stay the course, surviving more or less unchanged to the present day (though sometimes, like actors, taking involuntary 'rests' between assignments): Batman and Robin, Captain America, Wonder Woman, the Human Torch, the Sub-Mariner, Green Lantern, Green Hornet, Plastic Man . . . In the late Fifties and early Sixties, the Marvel Comics Group – playing Avis to rival D.C. Comics' Hertz under the masterful guidance of Stan 'the Man' Lee – introduced a further handful of characters who seem destined for permanent residence in the Comic Book Hall of Fame: Iron Man, Thor, Daredevil, Dr Strange, the Amazing Spiderman, the Incredible Hulk, the Fantastic Four. Bright, violent, innovative, introspective, studiously anarchic and surprisingly verbose, Marvel comics became as indispensable an element of Sixties' 'Youth culture' as the Beatles or Woodstock.

Comics being essentially a visual medium, a collection of superhero *fiction* such as the present book may strike some as being like a comic-book with everything removed except the word balloons! Yet superhero comics and Science Fiction (as these stories might most conveniently be described) have been inextricably entangled fellow-travellers since the beginning, influencing and sparking one another off all along the way. It might even be said that the superhero *genre* owes its very existence to Science Fiction since there are recognizable precedents for Superman in the written SF of the Thirties (quite apart from such obvious biblical and mythological antecedents as Samson, Hercules and Achilles etc.) In 1930 Philip Wylie's novel *Gladiator* introduced a proto-Superman named Hugh Donner, born super-strong, with bullet-resistant skin, as a result of his scientist father's experiments to produce a 'super-child'. Jerry Siegel, Superman's creator, reviewed *Gladiator* favourably in his own SF fanzine.

Then, in 1933, there began a long-running series of pulps (written by Lester Dent under the pen-name Kenneth Robeson) chronicling the adventures of *Doc Savage* – also known, on account of his unusual skin-colouring, as *The Man of Bronze*. Early advertisements for the series even described Doc as a Superman. In fact, Clark Savage Jr was a lot closer to what philosopher Frederich Nietzsche had in mind when he wrote about his idealistic concept of the Superman (or *Übermensch*) than was Siegel and Shuster's creation. Doc had to work hard at becoming a super-hero, doggedly pursuing a gruelling daily regime of exercises for physical and mental self-development. Compared to the Man of Bronze, the Man of Steel had it easy – he was simply *born* super!

The collaboration, conscious or otherwise, between SF and the comics has continued unabated since those pioneering days. Edmond Hamilton, Otto Binder, Manly Wade Wellman, Gardner Fox, Alfred Bester, Harry Harrison and Michael Moorcock are just some of the comic-book writers who became leading SF writers, or SF writers who have written for comic-books, bringing about a highly-desirable cross-fertilization of the two mediums.

And so to the stories in this collection of SUPER-HEROES.

Robert Bloch's *Stuporman* is a parody of 1943 vintage, one of a very entertaining series of Bloch stories about the misadventures of Lefty Feep, an incorrigible Forties Munchausen whose diction was Runyon and whose tales were taller than anyone else's. Feep's exploits often read like scenarios for unmade Marx Brothers' movies, and it's not hard to imagine Groucho taking the part of, say, Subconscious Sigmund in *Stuporman*.

As the title suggests, George E. Clark's *The Evil Super-Man* involves an attempt to create a superman who'll play on the bad guys' team for a change. The plot is straight out of the early horror comics (George E. Clark was a pseudonym of frequent pulp contributor Dale Clark, whose *oeuvre* includes stories with such delightful titles as *Lovers in a Tomb* and *My Friend – the Corpse*). And so too are the characters, who include a monster with a liking for well-cut suits and tearing off people's heads, and an egg-headed mad scientist who bears a disturbing resemblance to Captain Marvel's arch-enemy, Doctor Sivana. (If ever there was a special Nobel Prize for mad scientists, Dr Sivana – and not Superman's stolid adversary, Lothar – would surely run away with the award!) This story first appeared in *Marvel Tales*, a 1940 horror pulp, where it was intriguingly announced as 'a pulse-pounding novelette of young love – 1978 style!'

There are more mad lab shenanigans in *Origin of a Superhero* by Donald Glut, a well-known authority on comics and fantasy films who also writes for Marvel comics – *Captain America*, *Kull the Destroyer* and *Star Wars* are among the titles which he's recently scripted. (Coincidentally, Don had a lead part in an early film by George Lucas, writer and director of STAR WARS: the title, appropriately, was GLUT.) In his capacity as official family historian of the Frankenstein family, Don is also the author of *The Frankenstein Legend* and other related works – so it should come as no surprise that his story includes an appearance by one of those Rothschilds of the monster-making industry.

Female superheroes are relatively rare in both comics and SF but they do exist. April 1939 saw the publication in *Fantastic Adventures* of *The Golden Amazon*, the first in a series of stories by Thornton Ayre (alias prolific British SF writer John Russell Fearn) about Violet Ray, a girl of the future who gets shipwrecked on Venus as a child. Affected by the planet's alien atmosphere, Violet grows up to be a golden-skinned superwoman of superior strength and intellect – qualities which she soon learns to put to good effect in the fight against evil. One memorable characteristic of the Golden Amazon was the obvious relish with which she beat up members of the opposite sex. By the time of her third adventure, *The Golden Amazon Returns* (reprinted in this book), the tough-talking Amazon was happily married with a couple of kids to look after (maybe one reason why there aren't more female superheroes), but still found time to punch out the occasional male villain . . . In December 1941, two years after the original Golden Amazon adventure, another superheroine, Wonder Woman, made her debut appearance in *All Star Comics*. Wonder Woman was also described as an Amazon, had super-strength and super-intelligence, and derived equal pleasure from beating up men! Credit for the creation of *Wonder Woman* was claimed by Charles Moulton (alias psychologist William Moulton Marston), who also wrote the stories, and the strip was drawn by artist Harry Peter in an unattractive style that made most of the characters look like dumpy, muscle-bound puppets. In spite of its unappealing appearance (the present TV-influenced *Wonder Woman* is less eccentrically drawn) the strip caught on and has remained successful to this day.

Captain Amazing by Stephen Hitchcock introduces

another extra-terrestrial superhero, one whose single-handed war against bullion thieves is not quite the public-spirited crusade everyone thinks it is.

John A. Keel's *Satyr-Man* might equally be called 'Satire-Man' since the story mischievously lampoons an incompetent superhero, not unlike a certain caped crusader . . . Sensitive souls beware! – it's a ribald, X-rated parody, closer in spirit (and body) to Flesh Gordon than Flash Gordon.

Adrian Cole's amusing tale of *Transmuto, the Metamorphic Myrmidon* reminds me a lot of Jack Cole's *Plastic Man*, one of the funniest and most imaginative strips ever to appear between covers. Transmuto actually has it one better than Plastic Man. Plas could stretch or contract his weird red and yellow body into all kinds of extraordinary shapes, but he never was able to take on the form of another living creature the way Transmuto can.

Easy Way Out by Marion Pitman suggests what comics might be like if reality was ever allowed to supercede the Comics' Code. Or if superheroes ceased to honour the Marquis of Queensberry.

During the sixties there was a trend (initiated by Marvel Comics) towards making superheroes more 'human' by weighing them down with all sorts of petty, mundane, personal problems such as we mere mortals have to contend with. For a while, characters like Spiderman seemed more preoccupied by such matters of Earth-shaking import as bad marks at school, broken dates, how to pay the rent and what they were going to have for dinner than by the impending destruction of the known universe at the eight (count 'em!) slimy hands of Doc Octopus and his ilk! George Alec Effinger's *The Awesome Menace of 'The Polarizer'*, one of a continuing series of stories about a Marvel-style hero called the Iguana, reflects something of this existential phase – while Allan Kimball's *Up, Up and Away* carries it on through to the bitter end. In Norman Spinrad's *It's a Bird, It's a Plane*, even Clark Kent, finally unbalanced by the strain of maintaining a dual identity, is driven to seek the services of a psychiatrist.

Frank Adey's *Alternative Ending* is exactly that.

Finally, *Man of Steel, Woman of Kleenex* by Larry Niven is not fiction at all but a penetrating piece of investigative journalism that Lois Lane herself would be proud to have written (and who better qualified than she?) With a thoroughness that leaves absolutely nothing to the imagination, everything you always wanted to know about Superman's sex-life (but were much too well brought up to ask) is fearlessly revealed – including the real reason the Man of Steel is so rusty when it comes to girls.

Twelve superheroes *and* the secrets of Superman's private life revealed . . . If this book doesn't get you putting on a mask and secret underwear and swinging out the nearest window to do battle with the forces of evil – then there's no hope for you.

'Nuff said: It's *clobbering* time!

Michel Parry, 1978

Stuporman

by Robert Bloch

If it hadn't been that I was dying of hunger, I never would have stuck my nose into Jack's Shack. It really isn't safe to stick your nose into that restaurant, because you are liable to smell some of the food.

But there was another reason why I hesitated.

Down at one of the tables, I saw the tall, angular figure of Mr Lefty Feep. He was leaning against the back of a chair with a great air of business about him – other people's business, as usual.

I was afraid he might see me and come over, and for certain reasons I wished to avoid meeting him. Because when you meet Lefty Feep he talks to you, and when he talks to you, you listen, and if you listen, you'll hear something that will distress you for days.

However, I was pleased to see that Feep was already attached to a victim – a little thin man with eyeglasses and a nervous expression. He was talking to the small, bespectacled stranger quite earnestly, and the stranger was listening. I didn't recognize the fellow, but I felt sorry for him. It grieved me to see that he had a bandage around his head, but it grieved me more to see the way Feep was talking to him. I knew what suffering he was going through.

I tiptoed over to a table. Feep didn't look up. I called the waiter. Feep was still talking. I gave my order. Feep gabbled on. My food came, and I ate. Feep was rattling away.

I grinned. This was one time I'd get away scot-free. I laid a tip on the tablecloth and rose to go.

'Do not scurry in such a hurry.'

The voice of Lefty Feep cut through my complacency. I looked up. The one-man crime wave against the English language was standing at my table. He sat down.

I sat down, too, when he pushed me into a chair.

'You must please believe that I grieve when I do not perceive you until you are about to leave,' announced Feep, picking up a toothpick and signalling the waiter for a glass of water.

'I'm sorry, Lefty,' I answered. 'But I must be off.'

'Never mind your mental condition,' he smiled. 'I want to talk to you.'

'But I must go now.'

'Kindly do not bring up biological problems,' Feep insisted. 'I see you are wearing your golf socks today.'

I glanced down at my feet.

'Golf socks?' I echoed.

'Yes,' said Feep. 'The ones with the eighteen holes.'

I rose again. 'Listen, Lefty, I have no time to waste listening to your insults. Why don't you go over and bore that fellow you were talking to before?'

Feep caught my coat-tails and pulled me down again.

'You notice that personality?' he asked. 'The little skinny guy with the goggles?'

'Of course I noticed him. Who is he?'

'Who is he?' gasped Feep. 'You mean to inform me you do not recognize him?'

'No.'

'Why, that is none other than Joe Blow.'

'Joe Blow?'

'The famous Stuporman.'

'Who in the world is Stuporman?' I asked.

'Why, I always figure everybody knows who Stuporman is,' Feep sighed.

I shook my head.

'Well,' said Feep, 'I will tell his story, if you insist.'

'I don't insist.'

'You are just being polite,' said Lefty Feep. 'It is such a yarn as is not unravelled every day. Kindly lend me your ears and I will bend them for you.'

He did.

With a lightning flick of his tongue, Lefty Feep began his tale.

When I first hear of this personality, Joe Blow, he is a reporter on *The Daily Bulb*, a news-bladder. I see him hanging around Gorilla Gabface's pool palace oncely or twicely, and when I examine this specimen of manhood I am more depressed than impressed.

Joe Blow is a little insignificant jerk who is too weak to lick his own lips.

I hear from some of the downtown boys that he is not a very good reporter, and he is always having trouble. It seems Joe is very much in a fatuated condition over a beautiful girl reporter by the name of Effie Fink.

But Effie Fink does not yearn and burn for Joseph Blow. She thinks he is a sissy. First his draft board turns him down and then his girl friend turns him down. In fact, he gets turned down oftener than the lamp in the parlour of a sailor's girl-friend.

Joe Blow is also turned down around the mouth when I meet him on the street one day. He recognizes me from the pool hall and ambles over with a sad, unglad smile.

'Hello, Joe,' I greet him. 'What's heating for eating? What, I inquire, is on the fire? In a word, what's cooking?'

'My goose,' answers Joe Blow, very mournful.

'You have troubles?'

'Like Mussolini,' sighs Joe. 'I will live in a hotel for five years, and the manager rents my nice room to somebody else and gives me a bum room instead.'

'Bum room? That's bad.'

'I have worse,' sighs Joe Blow. 'My editor also gives me the bum's rush. On top of that, the other fellows at the paper are always picking on me. And to finish it all off, my girl friend, Effie Fink, is running around with a racketeer.'

I sympathize with this little runt. 'You must assert

yourself,' I tell him. 'You must be impressive and aggressive.'

'Just look at me,' sobs Joe Blow. 'I could not be more run-down if I would get hit by a truck.'

'Why not take some vitamins?' I suggest.

Joe Blow shakes his head. 'I am too weak to swallow them,' he tells me. 'Besides, they take too long to do any good. I must work fast to regain my girl-friend, also my self-respect.'

'How about a muscle course?' I inquire.

He shakes his head again.

'I send in for one, but they do not mail me my muscles yet.'

I try to console him. 'We should be able to think of something. With my brains and your troubles – wait a minute! Brains – troubles – I know just the thing for you to do!'

'Commit suicide?' asks Joe hopefully.

'Not at all,' I cackle. 'We will go to see the psychologist, Subconscious Sigmund. Any time you need your wits sharpened, he is the guy to grind your mind.'

'How can he help me?'

'He can psycho-analyze your condition. He can explain the pain in your brain.'

'Let's go,' says Joe Blow.

So we do. I steer him up to Subconscious Sigmund's office in the quickest kind of a hurry.

We walk inside and see Subconscious Sigmund talking on the telephone, but he nods for us to sit down and wait.

I gather that Sigmund is phoning a barber shop because his kid needs a haircut.

'Let me know when two barbers are free,' he says, hanging up.

'Why does your kid need two barbers for a haircut?' I ask.

'The kid has two heads,' says Subconscious Sigmund. 'And now, what can I do for you?'

I point to Joe Blow and introduce him. 'I wish you to tell me what is numb with his skull,' I request.

So Sigmund takes Joe Blow into his private office and gives him the third degree. He pumps him for his life history. He grills him like a weenie.

Joe Blow is soon pouring out all his troubles.

Subconscious Sigmund listens very carefully.

'Do you ever dream?' he asks.

'Of course I do.'

'What about?'

'Oh, I don't know,' says Joe Blow, kind of embarrassed. 'I have very peculiar dreams. I dream that I am strong, powerful, dynamic. I can lift great weights and have remarkable endurance. I have the ability to see through walls, and hear any sound. And in some dreams I can even fly.'

'Aha!' says Subconscious Sigmund.

'Also,' says Joe Blow, blushing, 'in some dreams I am always having dates with movie queens.'

'Really,' says Subconscious Sigmund. 'You are strong, powerful, forceful, eh? And you have dates with movie queens.'

'That's right,' says Joe Blow. 'Can you do anything to help me?'

'Sure,' snaps Subconscious Sigmund. He fumbles around and hands Blow a little white box.

'What's this?' asks Blow.

'A box of sleeping tablets,' grunts Subconscious Sigmund. 'With dreams like that, what do you want to stay awake for?'

Joe Blow sighs, puts the box in his pocket, and plods downstairs. I follow him.

'Do not be discouraged,' I remark, when we hit the street. 'I have another idea that might help you.'

'Nothing can help me.'

'Rome wasn't burned in a day,' I tell him. 'We will try again. I think we ought to go over and see Skeetch and Meetch.'

'Who?'

'Sylvester Skeetch and Mordecai Meetch,' I answer. 'The famous scientific Americans. They run the *Horsecracker Institute*, and they are always inventing stuff in their laboratory, such as new ways to avoid paying the rent.'

'Can they help me?'

'If anybody can, they are the personalities,' I brag. 'They are scientific, but terrific.'

So Joe Blow trims his limbs over towards the *Horsecracker Institute*.

We climb the stairs to the big private laboratory where Skeetch and Meetch hang out, mostly around the elbows.

Little fat Skeetch and his chubby partner glare over their goggles in the outer office when we come in.

'Lefty Feep!' yells Skeetch. 'It's a pleasure to see you! Sit down! Have a cigar? Good – then give it to me!'

'I want to read you my latest monograph,' Meetch interrupts. 'It is entitled "AN APPREHENSION OF AN INTENTION FOR THE PREVENTION OF INVENTION" and it just won an Honorable Mention at the Convention.'

'I haven't time,' I tell them. 'I only come here because I bring you a case.'

'Open it up and I will get the glasses,' says Skeetch.

'Not it – him,' I correct, pointing at Joe Blow.

'What do you want us to do – bury him?' inquires Skeetch.

'No. I want you to listen to his story and help him.'

So Joe Blow gives out with a pout about his fate. He tells about his bum room, his overbearing editor, his reporter friends that pick on him, and his girl friend who runs around with a racketeer. He mentions that he is weak and meek and the future looks bleak.

Skeetch and Meetch sigh and shake their heads.

I can see they don't know what to suggest.

But Joe Blow goes on. He tells about seeing Subconscious Sigmund, and answering questions about his dreams. He mentions dreaming of flying and being strong and dynamic.

Suddenly both Skeetch and Meetch jump up and yell.

'We have it!' yells Meetch. 'Eureka!'

'So do you,' I snap.

'You come at the right moment,' Skeetch babbles. 'We are just looking for a subject to experiment on with our new machine.'

'Machine? What do you mean?'

'The most keen machine you've ever seen!' raves Meetch. 'We call it the *Morpheus Arm*.'

'Why?'

'Because it works while you sleep. It is a mechanical hypnotic device which translates the subconscious images of dreams into waking realities, utilizing subliminal concepts and energizing the psychic trauma until a vitalization occurs which impinges imaginative free-fantasies upon a framework of actuality, thus setting up a basis of positive activity actuated by the psyche.'

'The hell you tell,' I exclaim.

'What does he mean?' asks Joe Blow.

'Why it is simple,' I inform him. 'He means he invents a machine that turns your sleeping thoughts into waking realities. Whatever you imagine you can do while you dream, you actually can do.'

'Right,' says Meetch. 'I couldn't explain it better myself. In fact, I couldn't explain it.'

'But how does this machine operate?' persists Blow.

'Very simple arrangement,' says Skeetch. 'The subject goes to sleep. As he sleeps, electro-magnetic impulses, due to photo-electronic control are set up. The subject's heart action is synchronized to the movement of the machine. At the same time, a hypnotic force draws bodily magnetism from the sleeper as he dreams. The dreams, in a word, become a part of the machine – and the energy of the machine, operating in ratio with the dream image, flows into the body of the sleeper.

'When the sleeper wakes up, he has the ability and strength to carry out his dream activities. Simple?'

'You are simple,' I tell him. 'It sounds screwy to me.'

'The machine is in our laboratory now,' protests Meetch.

'I'd like to look at it, anyway,' sighs Joe Blow. So we drag into the big laboratory.

Sure enough, there is this huge arm, attached to a big black cluster of wheels and wires, mounted on a heavy metal base set above an operating table.

'Looks like they've got something here,' says Joe Blow.

'Yeah – something for the scrap drive,' I sneer.

'I believe these gentlemen,' says Joe Blow. 'I think I would like to make the experiment. After all, what have I got to lose? I am down and out. But if I could be the way I am in my dreams – oh boy!'

'All you need to do is go to sleep,' says Skeetch.

I shrug. If that is what Joe Blow wants, he will have it. But I cannot wait around for him to go to sleep.

Still, I am always glad to do a friend a favour.

So I walk behind Joe Blow and tap him over the head with a hammer.

He falls asleep at once.

Skeetch and Meetch lift him up on the table. He lies there under the laboratory lights, looking weaker and skinnier and littler than ever.

Skeetch and Meetch go into their act. They indulge in a lot of wire-connecting, strap-buckling, switch-fiddling, button-pressing, and assorted dial-turning.

All at once the machinery begins to hum in various keys, like the Four Ink Spots. Then it gains a little power and begins to sing, off-key, like the Andrews Sisters.

Sylvester Skeetch and Mordecai Meetch swing the big arm of the machine over until it hangs just above Joe Blow's head. The arm jiggles up and down. A little screen in back of the machine base lights up and long streaks of electricity crackle across it.

The pinball operators will pay real money for stuff like this, I figure.
But Skeetch and Meetch are more of the screwball operator type.
All at once Meetch utters a mutter.
'It isn't working right,' he says. 'We can't synchronize the heart action because the patient's pulse is too weak.'
'Adrenalin,' suggests Skeetch. He runs over to a glass cabinet and comes back with a hypodermic needle.
'Let's go,' yells Meetch. 'Shoot the harpoon to me, goon.'
They give Joe Blow the needle.
The machine begins to groan and shake. So does Joe Blow. But in rhythm with the machine!
Now I notice the electric streaks on the screen also move in rhythm with Joe Blow's breathing. Everything is synchronized. And the arm above Joe Blow's head seems to be conducting energy from the machine into his body.
I sit there watching, and eating a banana, with rapt scientific curiosity. What will happen next? A short-circuit, I suspect.
But there is no explosion.
All at once the two geniuses rush over to Joe Blow and unstrap him. Meetch goes over to a wash stand and comes back with a glass of water which he throws in Joe Blow's face.
Joe Blow wakes up, sits up, gets up.
He is awake, and that is no fake.
I stare at him. He doesn't look any different as he climbs off the table.

In back of him the machine grinds away, but that is the only evidence that anything happens during the last ten minutes. Except for that, it might all be a dream.
But if you ever see a dream walking, it is Joe Blow – as I soon discover.

'How do you feel?' I yell, above the machine's humming noise.

He smiles.

'Wonderful! Marvellous! Superb! Not so bad!' he announces.

Skeetch rushes up to him.

'It's a success,' he gasps. 'The machine works! Congratulations for helping our experiment.'

He shakes hands with Joe Blow. Suddenly he starts to scowl and howl.

'Ouch!' yells Skeetch. 'Leggo – you're breaking my fingers!'

Joe Blow lets go. He takes off his glasses and throws them away.

'Don't need these any more,' he announces.

We look at him, wondering if it is true.

'My friend,' says Meetch, 'if you benefit from this machine, we are very happy. As long as it continues to operate you will be living your dreams. We will not shut if off. So if you are indeed stronger and more capable due to our efforts we are very pleased. We urge you to take full advantage of the machine's powers, so we can study the effects. In a word, make your dreams come true.'

Joe Blow stands there. He is still a little, scrawny-looking guy, but he has a new smile on his face.

'Very well, gentlemen,' he says. 'Thank you for all your trouble. But if you will pardon me,' he murmurs, 'I must go now.'

'Goodbye, Joe,' I tell him.

'Goodbye,' says Joe Blow, stepping over to the open window and flying away into the night.

Yes that is exactly what he does! He marches to the open window and hurls himself through the air like a rocket.

'For sobbing out loud!' I yell. 'Look at that!'

Skeetch blinks, but Meetch winks.

'That's what he dreams about,' he tells me. 'With the aid of the machine he should be able to do that. He is almost walking – or rather, flying – in his sleep now. His brain is awake, but his soul is in a sort of a stupor.'

'Stuporman,' says Skeetch.

'Exactly,' Meetch answers. 'Joe Blow is now a Stuporman. As long as we keep our machine running, he can do whatever his imagination will allow.'

Skeetch rubs his hands. 'Well, that's that,' he says. 'We will let the machine run awhile and see what happens to our subject in this little experiment. But now we must go back to work. What is next on our programme, Meetch?'

Meetch looks at his list.

'We are supposed to build a rocket-ship,' he announces.

'All right,' says Skeetch. 'I suppose it will take us several days, at least. You had better go now, Lefty.'

So I take my leave of Skeetch and Meetch, wondering all the while what Joe Blow does after he flies off into the night.

I do not find out until a long time afterwards. But this is the way it works out.

Joe Blow is very delighted to find he can fly. He glides along over the rooftops, hoping an Army patrol doesn't spot him, and practises gliding and swooping and dipping, and maybe a little peeking into second-storey windows.

But after a while the novelty wears off and Joe Blow realizes he has a job to do.

So he heads over to his hotel. He lights down in the alley in back and walks in very normally. He prances up to the desk, where the manager is sitting – a fat, tough-looking number.

'Pardon me,' he coughs, looking meek.

'Why should I?' growls the manager, looking up. He is the fellow who imposes on Joe Blow by kicking him out of his good room and putting him in a cubbyhole a few days before.

'I should like to have my old room back,' Blow remarks.

The manager glares. 'I already tell you it is quite impossible. That room is rented to somebody else now.'

'But it has a nice southern exposure,' argues Joe Blow. 'I lived in it for five years and like it. Now you transfer me to a little closet with no windows at all. What can I do for air?'

'You can get the hell out of here,' suggests the manager. 'I have no time to waste arguing with an insignificant little pip-squeak like you.'

Joe Blow shrugs. 'No southern exposure?' he mumbles. 'All right. Suit yourself.'

He walks out of the hotel. The manager laughs.

But a minute later, the manager is not laughing. He is shaking. In fact, the whole building is shaking.

The shaking turns to a terrific shudder. Then there is a rumble, a totter, the building seems to lift in the air, and everything whirls around.

When the manger opens his eyes again, everything is quiet. And normal.

He rushes to the door and looks outside to see about the earthquake.

He looks around and almost collapses.

'I'm on the wrong street!' he whispers.

The explanation, of course, is simple. Joe Blow wants a room with southern exposure. So he merely goes outside and lifts up the building and turns it around until his room faces south.

Then he puts it back down, punches a hole through the wall of his room for a window, and flies away.

'This Stuporman business is all right,' he thinks to himself, lighting on the pavement across from his newspaper office.

He starts to cross the street.

A car whizzes around the corner, almost clipping him. A tough but gruff voice sings out, 'Whyn'cha look where youse is going, huh? Wanna hold up traffic?'

Ordinarily, Joe Blow cringes when somebody yells at him. But now he yells right back.

'Yes, I do want to hold up traffic,' he says.

And he scoops up the car in his arms and holds it up. He puts it down out of his way, and crosses the street.

The tough but gruff guy is now sick but quick.

Joe Blow ignores him and marches into the newspaper office. He heads straight for the back where the editor hangs out.

Usually he does not dare to invade his privacy, but today he walks right into the inner office and sits down.

The editor looks up.

'So here you are, eh, Blow? What the hell's been keeping you?' he snarls.

'It's my day off.'

'Day off? Day off? You just have a day off last week when your appendix busts.'

'I know, but—'

'Listen, Blow,' snarls the editor. 'While you are taking your day off, stories are breaking all over town. I get a report about some nut who is flying over the city. Do you phone me in the yarn? No!'

'I can explain—'

'Shuddup! Then the manager of the hotel down the street phones in about an earthquake. It picks up his hotel and turns it around on its foundations. Do you cover this story? No!'

'But listen, sir—'

'You know what I'm gonna do, Blow?' yells the editor, getting up and grabbing Blow by the scruff of his neck. 'I'm gonna kick you out.'

And he aims a very hearty kick indeed at Joe Blow's stomach while his back is turned.

'Ouch!' moans the editor, hopping around and grabbing his foot. 'What you got – lead in your pants?'

Joe Blow pushes the editor back into a chair and smiles.

'Now *you* listen to *me*,' he says.

The editor sits back very quiet. He is so quiet you can hear his eyes popping when Joe Blow exhibits his new personality as Stuporman.

'I am sick and tired of your bossing,' says Blow. 'For ten years I work here on the *Daily Bulb* without a raise. I think it is about time you double my salary.'

'What the—'

'Sit down!' snaps Blow. 'I am not afraid of you any more, you big yard of lard. You are not as tough as you look. For a while I think you are all muscle, but now I know your secret. Do I get the raise, or do I tell all the reporters you wear a corset?'

'Corset?' screams the editor. 'How do you know – are you the devil?'

'No,' says Joe Blow. 'But my super-vision tells me that beneath your vest is a corset.'

The editor blushes. He shakes his head violently.

'Don't be upset,' Blow adds. 'Your wig will slide off.'

The editor gulps.

'We all know you wear a wig,' Blow tells him. 'Matter of fact, my super-hearing tells me that some of the reporters in the outer office are talking about it right now. They are wondering if you ever find any eggs in that bird-nest you have on your head.'

The editor, after screaming, blushing, and gulping, is too tired to do anything. He just sits there.

'Where do you get your wonderful hearing and vision?' he inquires. 'To say nothing of whatever you have when I try to kick you?'

'Never mind,' Joe Blow cracks. 'From now on I will not be taking kicks any more, I will be giving them out. And you are always at the top of my list.'

Blow grins. 'Yes sir,' he says. 'I have a deep-seated affection for you and—'

Just then the door opens and Blow's super-vision and super-hearing get a real workout. For into the room steps his girl-friend, Effie Fink. This damsel is really quite an eyeful and quite high-spirited. In fact she is all curves and nerves.

Joe Blow's mouth hangs open and he forgets all about his abilities as Stuporman.

Effie Fink ignores him and prances up to the editor.

'I think I'm on the trail of that subway graft,' she announces. 'The *Daily Bulb* will have a scoop tomorrow if your little girl reporter knows anything about it.'

'Fine,' says the editor. 'We ought to uncover this affair. We must find out what's holding up the subway construction.'

'I'm following a hot lead,' says Effie. 'Hope I don't get my nose burned.'

Joe Blow sits there gulping and hoping Effie Fink will notice him, but she doesn't.

'Ah – uh – hello, Effie,' he yammers.

Effie turns and gives him a look straight from the Deep-Freeze.

'Oh, it's you,' she remarks.

'Sure,' says Joe. 'Don't you notice me when you come in?'

'No,' answers the girl reporter. 'And I still don't.'

'Uh – how about going out with me this evening?'

Effie laughs.

'I'm sorry, but I already have an engagement, thank heaven! I am the guest of Mr Cutter.'

'You mean "Throats" Cutter, the racketeer?' gasps Joe.

'Never mind the vulgar nicknames. Mr Cutter is a gentleman, as far as I know, and I will thank you not to cast any aspersions on him.'

'I would like to cast something more than aspersions on that big baboon!' mutters Blow.

The damsel laughs. 'You? Why you haven't the strength enough to cast a vote,' she titters. 'But I cannot waste time. I'm on my way.'

Effie Fink breezes, banging the door shut behind her.

The editor looks at Joe Blow sitting there and trying to pick his face up from the floor when it starts falling.

'Huh!' grunts the editor. 'You and your super-vision and super-hearing and super-strength! Why don't you assert yourself with her, you super-chump?'

Joe Blow shakes his head. 'You don't understand,' he says. 'When I see Effie I don't think about myself any more. I forget everything. I worship the ground her open-toed shoes toddle on! Besides, I don't want her to know about my power. I want her to love me for myself.'

The editor has a slight change of heart. 'Don't feel so bad, Joe,' he advises. 'I happen to know she really doesn't like this "Throats" Cutter she hangs around with lately. It is merely that she suspects him of being mixed up in this graft to halt construction on the subway. She goes out with him to pump him, try to uncover the deal, and get a story for the paper.'

Joe Blow perks up a little when he hears this. 'I see,' he exclaims. 'It's strictly business.'

'Exactly. And this subway scandal is important.'

'Right,' says Joe Blow. 'Today I happen to be visiting my scientific friends, Skeetch and Meetch,' he observes, proudly. 'I notice that when the subway is completed it will end very close to their *Horsecracker Institute*.'

The editor makes a suggestion. 'Why don't you get on this story too?' he asks. 'The sooner we find out about the subway, the sooner Effie Fink is through with "Throats" Cutter.'

Joe Blow is so excited he forgets about his super-strength. He springs to his feet and bumps his head against the ceiling. He comes down gracefully, along with a shower of plaster.

'I'll do it,' he shouts. 'I'll follow her.'

'Probably she is at his apartment,' suggests the editor.

'In that racketeer's apartment? I must be off,' yells Blow.

He runs to the open window.

Blow blows.

The editor watches him dive out.
'Yes, he must be off,' he sighs.
But Joe Blow, flying through the night, is very much on. He swoops down at a corner drugstore and rockets into a phone booth. Every ounce of his new super-energy is quivering with excitement. He calls the *Horsecracker Institute*, meanwhile tearing the telephone book in half just for practice.
'Hello,' he yells, when Skeetch answers the phone. 'This is Joe Blow. Have you still got the *Morpheus Arm* working? Good! Be sure to keep it on. I'll need everything I've got tonight.'
He hangs up, whirls through the drugstore, and takes off from the kerb.
A cop sees him flying into the night.
'Hey, you!' he hollers. 'Why don't you wait until the lights change?'
But Joe Blow is already a mile up, zooming for the big apartment where 'Throats' Cutter hangs his coat and gat.
In a moment he is perched on the window ledge outside the 19th floor, using his super-vision to squint through into the rooms beyond.
There is Effie Fink, sitting on the sofa with 'Throats' Cutter. Joe Blow looks at the celebrated racketeer and shudders.
'Throats' Cutter is only about five feet six and weighs about 150 pounds, but he is every inch a thoroughbred. A thoroughbred rat. Even if his height and weight are only average, he looks very strong. His arms bulge with muscles and his hip-pockets bulge with hardware. He is sitting with his legs crossed, and Joe Blow can see a stiletto parked in his left stocking. He has his coat off and is relaxing in a bullet-proof vest, but his tie is neatly knotted to hide the blackjack hanging underneath it. 'Throats' Cutter is smoothing back his coal-black hair with his left hand, because his right hand is covered with brass knuckles.

Effie Fink doesn't seem to notice this one-man arsenal's appearance. She is giving him the old oil.

'It must be marvellous to be so important,' she sighs. 'And have so many people interested in you.'

'I get shot at every day,' says Cutter, proudly.

'You must be very busy,' whispers the damsel. 'I hear you are interested in the new subway.'

'Who tells you that?' snaps Cutter, his eyes glittering like the teeth on a hungry shark.

'Oh, a little birdie.'

'A little dead birdie, if I ever catch him,' mutters Cutter.

'But isn't it true?' needles the girl reporter.

'Don't bother your head about such things and you'll keep it longer,' says Cutter. 'Wait a minute. I'll mix us up a drink and we'll get sociable.'

He gets up and walks out very slow, because of all the hardware weighing him down.

Effie Fink doesn't waste any time. The minute he leaves the room she runs to the desk, trying the drawers. They are locked. Then she runs over to the wall safe and fiddles with it. It doesn't open.

Finally she sees a closet door and opens it.

In the closet hangs three overcoats, two suits, and a large man with a bandage in his mouth.

'Eeeeek!' remarks Effie Fink.

She turns around. 'Throats' Cutter stands in the doorway of the parlour, watching her.

'Do not be alarmed,' he says, smiling. 'He is doing all right hanging there in the closet. I have insect spray in there so the moths won't get him.'

'But I know him,' the girl reporter blurts. 'That's Ambrose Reed, the contractor who is building the subway.'

'Not any more,' grins Cutter. 'From now on I am building the subway.'

'You kidnap him?' whispers the girl.

Cutter doesn't grin any more.

'It is too bad you open that door,' he says. 'Because I do not like for people to discover the skeletons in my closet. Even big fat skeletons like this Ambrose Reed.'

'What are you going to do?' asks Effie Fink.

'I am going to tell you everything,' Cutter answers. 'Yes, I kidnap Ambrose Reed last week. I take over the contracting job and stir up trouble with the men so the work slows down. Because the longer it takes to build the subway, the more it costs. And the more it costs, the more I will make. Understand?'

'Yes.' Effie frowns. 'But why do you admit all this to me?'

Cutter laughs. 'So you will have a good story to put in the paper tomorrow, of course,' he answers.

'You mean I can print it?'

Cutter shrugs. 'Well – maybe not. I think I've got a better story figured out. With a little female interest in it, see? How does this sound? "BEAUTIFUL GIRL REPORTER FOUND DEAD IN SUBWAY. IDENTITY UNKNOWN, BUT SEARCHERS ARE CONFIDENT OF FINDING MORE BITS SHORTLY AND PUTTING THEM TOGETHER." There's a real story, eh?'

It is a trifle difficult for Effie to answer this question, because she is now hanging upside down over Cutter's shoulder as he grabs her up and smothers her mouth with his hand.

He heads for the door and dashes out of the apartment by a rear elevator.

Joe Blow, meanwhile, is very busy on his own hook. Naturally, he wants to save Effie Fink from death.

But once a reporter, always a reporter. There is a big news story here, and he must get a scoop.

So as soon as Cutter and the damsel leave the room, he springs through the window and unties Mr Ambrose Reed.

In a flash he whips out a pencil and notebook and gets the story of his untimely snatching from the kidnapped contractor.

Then Stuporman's strength comes into play. He rips open the desk drawers and tears the safe door from the wall. He scoops out all the documents about the subway contracts.

In a twinkling he calls the editor of the *Daily Bulb* and delivers his lead story.

'Reed says this delay will hold up the subway six months,' he says. 'Yes, Reed's safe, with me. Effie Fink? Oh, Effie Fink is with Cutter at the subway. He's going to blow her to bits or something. What? I should save her? Not a bad idea.'

Joe Blow, the Stuporman, hangs up, waves goodbye to Ambrose Reed, and jumps out of the window.

'Dammit!' he yells, outside. 'I should have enough sense to open the window before I jump.'

But there is no time for quibbling. Joe Blow therefore, does not quibble. He flies. He heads for the dark, yawning mouth of the unfinished subway tunnel.

He swoops down into the black pit and skims along through darkness.

Far ahead a light gleams along the tracks.

In the glow, Joe Blow can see a sight that has not been his privilege to witness since the days of the silent movies.

Effie Fink is lying on the subway rails in the tunnel way beyond. She is tied hand and foot, and looks very uncomfortable.

Coming towards her is a big electric hand-car, whizzing along the rails. On the hand-car is a large keg of TNT, with the fuse sputtering away and burning down.

When it hits Effie Fink in a second or two, there will be a difficult time finding enough left of her to please a jigsaw fan.

This situation alarms Effie quite a bit, and she is uttering loud cries of displeasure.

Way down the tracks stands 'Throats' Cutter, and he does not agree with Effie Fink's complaints. He is laughing in a jolly fashion – a jolly fashion for a hyena, that is.

Joe Blow, *alias* Stuporman, takes in this situation with a single super-vision.

In one second the TNT and the hand-car will strike Effie Fink.

He hurls himself forward.

Fast as he is, he is still a hundred feet away.

Too late!

Mustering up every ounce of his strength, Stuporman opens his mouth, takes careful aim at the dynamite keg a hundred feet away – and spits the fuse out!

It sputters and dies, but the hand-car rolls.

Stuporman waits until it actually touches Effie Fink – so that the wheels cut the ropes tying her, and that saves him the trouble.

Then he zooms down and pushes the car back up the track. He gives it a powerful shove and it begins to rocket back towards 'Throats' Cutter. Cutter can't run away. He fumbles in the darkness of the tunnel and whirls around as the hand-car approaches with Stuporman sitting on it.

Joe Blow sees what Cutter has in his hands.

A big, black-barrelled sub-machine gun.

And it is aimed at him.

Stuporman or no Stuporman, he doesn't think he can stop bullets.

So as Cutter shoots, Stuporman Blow leaps up, comes down on the barrel of the gun, and bends it backwards while Cutter is firing it.

The bullets enter Mr Cutter very rapidly, and he becomes very dead.

Effie Fink comes running up, after taking all this time to pull up her stockings and put on fresh make-up.

'Oh, Joe, you're wonderful!' she whispers. 'You will be a hero for saving the subway.'

Joe Blow, the Stuporman, frowns.

'The subway!' he mutters. 'That's right. I know I forget something.'

'What is it, darling?' asks Effie Fink.

'Get out of here,' orders the new Joe Blow. 'I've got work to do.'

Meekly, Effie Fink walks up the tunnel and out of the unfinished subway at the nearest exit.

Joe Blow turns to the wall of earth beyond.

He glances at his wristwatch and sighs.

'Gosh! It's almost midnight. Well, that leaves me a couple of hours, anyway.'

So taking off his coat, Stuporman gets to work and finishes building the subway before morning!

Yes, all night long he tunnels and digs, and hauls and props and scoops and cements and pushes through under the streets.

By six a.m. he is dizzier than a cross-eyed octopus in a Hall of Mirrors.

Even Stuporman gets tired.

And that, of course, must be why he gets so confused and makes a mistake. His super-vision is reading blue prints while his super-strength is burrowing through the cement to build the terminal station.

Right then and there he goes wrong.

He digs a little too far and a little off-side.

As a matter of fact, he comes up in the basement of a building. The building above him is shaking and he hears familiar voices cursing away.

'What's the matter?' he croaks hoarsely. 'What's happening? Why do I feel so weak?'

After starting this quiz programme with himself, Joe Blow takes one look around him, gulps, and falls flat on his face.

When he wakes up he stares into the goggled eyes of Sylvester Skeetch and Mordecai Meetch.

'Why do you do it?' moans Meetch.

'Do what?' Joe Blow moans back at him.

'Dig up under our cellar and shake the building,'

Skeetch answers. 'When you do that you cause the *Morpheus Arm* to jiggle. It stops cold. Something goes wrong and it will not work any more!'

'You mean I wreck the machinery that controls my dreams come true?' sighs Joe Blow. 'I am not Stuporman any more?'

'No more,' says Skeetch.

'But you are a hero in today's papers,' Meetch consoles him.

Joe Blow gets up weakly.

'It's all over, I guess. Now I am just Joe Blow the reporter again. Effie Fink will not go for me now that I lose my superstrength.'

'Wait a minute,' Meetch suggested. 'Nobody needs to know you aren't Stuporman any more. Don't tell her. She will never catch on. Go to her now. I bet she will be your slave for life.'

Joe Blow takes this suggestion, nods, and beams. He walks out in the early morning sunshine with a smile on his face.

And sure enough, when he gets back to the office, Effie Fink falls all over him. The editor is proud, the subway contractor is overjoyed, and Joe Blow – the famous Stuporman – is a hero.

Lefty Feep finished wagging his tale and sat back.

I nodded.

'So that's how subways are built,' I said, a little sarcastically.

'Joe Blow tells me all about it himself just now,' Feep answered. 'You do not think he is a prevaricator, do you? And certainly you know that *I* am 100% truthful.'

'You're better than that,' I told Feep. 'Sometimes you're 200% at least.'

He smiled at the compliment.

I turned to stare at skinny little bespectacled Joe Blow.

'Seems hard to believe that such a runt could do so many wonderful things,' I sighed.

'You can see the subway for yourself. Doesn't that prove it?' Feep told me.

'I suppose so,' I admitted. 'But by the way, I forgot to ask you a question.'

'Let's have it,' said Lefty Feep.

'Why is your Stuporman friend wearing a bandage around his head?'

'Oh, that?'

Feep smiled as he replied.

'It seems he marries this girl Effie Fink, and she beats the hell out of him.'

The Evil Super-Man

by George E. Clark

CHAPTER I

BIRTH OF A SUPER-MAN

Graeme Mansfield repressed a slight shudder as he pushed the button beside the shining door of the scientist's laboratory. The wild, eager expression on Professor Thorndile's face, as it had appeared in the television mirror, and the uncontrolled squeak of his excited voice had prepared him for a distasteful half hour.

Mansfield was an artist; scientific matters bored him. He cheerfully admitted that he, like all humanity, profited every moment of his life from the discoveries of such men as this old professor. Yet even the projected flight to Mars, which after years of planning was scheduled to begin today, had failed to lure him from his glassite-domed studio, where he worked passionately over his own problem of the fourth-dimensional element in his latest painting, that of a superb golden goddess.

But old Thorndile had summoned him, pleadingly, and here he was.

They had nothing in common; in fact, he had found the scientist a rather irritating person. Nevertheless, despite his artistic sensitivity, he was tolerant of human shortcomings. If he disliked Thorndile, if there was something unusual, something slightly sinister in the professor's personality, Mansfield was ready to excuse it on the grounds of scientific preoccupation.

He pressed the button again. A blue light flared in his face from the mirror-like surface of the chromium steel door that guarded the scientist's sanctum. He was, he knew, visible to Professor Thorndile in his radionic-vision reflector, even though his own eyes could not pierce the steel partition. He frowned; it seemed strange that a man who took such precautions against unwelcome visitors should wish to see him.

The heavy door rolled back silently into the wall. Mansfield blinked his eyes. The laboratory appeared to be dark; but as he stepped forward he made out numerous reddish glows – ruby lights.

'Ha, you have come, my friend! Splendid, splendid!'

Professor Thorndile touched a button and some electrically controlled mechanism rolled the huge door shut behind Mansfield. Again he felt like shuddering.

He glanced around. The place had the atmosphere of a hell, to his sensitive imagination; he didn't enjoy the feeling of being locked in here. Everything had a reddish hue – the scientist's bald, egg-shaped head and lean face, with its sunken cheeks and eyes that peered at him through thick-lensed spectacles; his shrivelled old body; the walls and ceiling; the complex maze of benches, scales, test tubes and other paraphernalia – all tended to create a weird illusion, diabolically unreal.

'What is it you wish to tell me, Professor?' he asked, shaking the scientist's bony hand with attempted cordiality.

'Tell you! My friend, I got you here to *show* you, not tell you! I am about to reveal – for the first time to anyone but myself – the greatest miracle of scientific achievement since the year 1998! Do you know what outstanding discovery marked that year, Mansfield?'

'No,' the young man confessed, 'I'm afraid not. As you know, I'm an artist, not a scientist. I could tell you a number of advances that have been made in the field of art. For instance, in the ten years since 1998 the fourth-dimensional element, which I am now working on, was introduced into the works of Van Devere and Molct to a degree that makes our old conceptions—'

Professor Thorndile checked him.

'Art!' he scoffed. 'I know nothing of art – care nothing for it! I, Mansfield, am a scientist, the greatest scientific mind since Alterberg, the physicist, who gave the world his theory of eternitivity. I am even greater than Alterberg – as you shall be privileged to see for yourself!'

Mansfield avoided meeting the piercing gaze of those fanatical old eyes. As an artist, he had learned to be tolerant of the flaming ego-superiority of creative men. It was necessary, he supposed, for a man to have an exaggerated feeling of his own importance, at least privately, in order to put down all obstacles and accomplish the seemingly impossible. Even in this day of wonders, one who attempted radically new things had to contend with the incredulity of others. It was a race-instinct, apparently, to doubt whatever the imagination could not readily grasp. Yet Professor Thorndile's cackling voice and over-confident manner made him stir uncomfortably.

'Why have you chosen me, a layman, to be the first one to see this thing, whatever it is?' he asked, a trifle irritably.

'Ha, we will come to that later, my young friend! To understand, you must first view the miracle to which I am about to introduce you. Mansfield, my boy, the efforts of my hands and brain, of twenty-seven years of exhaustive study and toil, are today in the final stage of fulfilment! But, come – follow me!'

He led the way to a tall object which loomed up like a shrouded pillar in the semi-darkness. Then he jerked a cord, and the shroud arose, revealing what seemed to be a giant test tube.

'Look!' hissed the professor. 'What do you see?'

Mansfield pressed forward, straining his eyes. Dimly he could make out a network of wires, tubes, valves; a complication of tanks and wheels and agitators; and attached to the outside of the great test tube were numerous dials, regulators, indicators and moving graphs. He shook his head apologetically.

'What is it, Professor?' he asked politely, not wanting to appear rude by revealing his lack of interest.

The old man did not answer at once. He touched a switch, and soft rays of indirect light flooded the laboratory.

'Look again!' he urged.

Mansfield's indifferent gaze fell on the interior of the great glassite tube. He recoiled, gasping.

'Great Caesar – a *man*!'

Professor Thorndile chuckled. 'Yes, my friend, you are right! That fellow *is* a man, as much as yourself, but with a great difference. You, Mansfield, were born of a woman, in the normal orthodox fashion. This fellow—' He waved a hand to indicate his laboratory, then straightened his dwarfish body proudly. 'This fellow,' he said, 'is the product of my brain!'

Mansfield drew a deep breath, still staring. The creature was half floating in some kind of liquid. Mansfield dimly recalled having read somewhere that the mother's body provides her offspring only protection, water, food, oxygen; the embryo developing its own blood and tissue. This liquid, then, must be a blood-substitute containing oxygen and bacteria-destroying properties; the tube attached to the creature's navel supplied food. The rest – the flexible wires joined by suction caps to certain muscles, the tubes running to nose and mouth and ears, Mansfield did not understand. What amazed him most was the size of the supposed infant; he was at least eight feet in height!

'Robot?' Mansfield asked hoarsely.

'Robot!' the scientist mocked scornfully. His voice sent a little chill down Mansfield's spine. 'Would a robot have flesh and blood? Would it kick – would its heart beat? You, my young friend, are seeing a full-grown specimen of *homo sapiens*, scientifically developed!'

The artist's face showed his perplexed incredulity.

'Surely,' cried the scientist, 'you can see for yourself! Even a layman today knows that science has long been experimenting with the test tube baby! You must be aware, Mansfield, that to bring to birth rabbits and cats and dogs and cattle – even monkeys – outside the mother's body has become commonplace in the last decade! Only the human being, the most complicated of all vertebrates, has continued to defy that inevitable accomplishment!'

Mansfield roused himself out of his amazed stupor.

'The test tube baby!' he muttered, catching at the familiar phrase to steady himself. 'Yes, certainly. They've been talking about that for half a century. I've read how Colonel Lindbergh, away back in 1936, gave up aviation and began to experiment with the possibilities of developing an infant in a test tube. Yes, and everyone knows that Dr Leicester recently succeeded in bringing the Morrell sextuplets into the world after seven months in an incubator of some sort. But this—' He wiped his brow. 'This, Professor, is not a – *baby*!'

'Of course he's not a baby! He has the physical development of a thirty-year-old adult. See those radionic vibrators? They have produced in three years muscles that no human ever possessed before! And his brain! He has the intellect of a man of fifty, yet his mind has the plasticity, the teachableness of a young child! He will be known as the wonder of the age – of all time! Mansfield, you are looking at the long-awaited *superman* of this planet!'

Mansfield gasped.

'Did I not tell you that I am greater than even Alterberg?' cackled the scientist. 'What do you think now, heh?'

'I – I can scarcely credit my own eyes with the truth!' whispered Mansfield. 'I've learned to believe anything is possible to man's ingenuity, and yet—'

'And yet your eyes do not lie!' the old man chortled. 'When you learn the potentialities of my super-man, you will be still more amazed, my young friend. Do you know how old that fellow is? Four years old! I developed him from a mass of protoplasm to his present perfection in four years and eighteen days. Do you believe me?'

Mansfield tore his gaze from the quietly pulsating figure to look at the scientist. He felt a little faint, his brain reeled, his mind was staggered at what he was witnessing.

'Tell me,' he demanded hoarsely, 'how you did it! Is he – is he human?'

'Yes and no!' chuckled the old man, delighted at his guest's stupefaction. 'He is a controlled variation, just as the race of mankind is a nature-evolved variation from the ancient *Pithencanthropus erectus*, the once so-called missing link from the ape man to *homo sapiens*. If you were a scientist, Mansfield, I could readily make you understand a great deal. Do you know anything about embryology, histology, anatomy, morphology, physiology or psychology?'

Mansfield shook his head regretfully.

'Right now I wish I did,' he said. 'Of course my artistic training included elementary anatomy and physiology, and nowadays every layman knows a little psychology. But maybe I can grasp a little of what you say. How on earth did you—'

'I will explain, then, such scientific details as you can understand, but not yet. First, my friend, let us examine another wonder which my brain has created. To you, an artist, this one will be of extreme interest, no doubt, because—'

He checked himself, obviously unwilling to reveal his secret beforehand. They passed into another part of the laboratory, where Mansfield beheld another curtained test tube. Thorndile raised the shroud.

'Darkness has been essential to embryonic development,' he remarked, 'but now it does not matter. In a short time—' He glanced at his watch. 'In exactly fourteen minutes they will be ready to be born.'

'*They*.' Mansfield gaped at the test tube. 'Is this another?'

The professor moved a switch and again hidden lights flooded upon them. Mansfield caught his breath sharply, staring.

'A – woman!' he cried. 'A beautiful woman! Why, great Caesar.' His stare widened, incredulously. 'It's – *it's the golden goddess!*'

CHAPTER II

THE SECOND MIRACLE

Graeme Mansfield knew that he was looking at the most beautiful female his eyes had ever seen. Her mass of golden hair bore a striking resemblance to the hair he had tried to produce on his canvas; but a second glance disclosed that his conception had been far short of the matchless vision he was now staring at.

She was a young girl, apparently about eighteen or nineteen, according to normal standards. Mansfield in all his life had never seen such glorious physical perfection in any creature. The most ideal models who had ever posed for him were crude and ill-shaped in comparison with this girl. From the top of her golden head to the bottom of her shapely pink toes, which no shoe had ever marred, she was the acme of perfect womanhood.

Yet Mansfield realized sickeningly that she must be abnormal, like the giant super-man he had just seen. She had the same tubes at navel, nostrils, mouth and ears, though the muscle developers were missing from her shapely figure.

'She's not – not human – not normal, I mean, is she?'

he asked, feeling a sudden unreasoning hatred of the professor.

'Yes, she is,' Thorndile said. 'I have not experimented with her beyond the most elementary matters of embryonic culture. She is a fully developed girl, Mansfield, the equivalent of a twenty-year-old woman, but her great beauty makes her look younger. To me, she is of secondary importance. I have not cared to over-develop her, as she will serve my purpose in her normal state, with all its normal functions.'

'Your purpose?' echoed Mansfield. 'What purpose?'

'I was referring to the part she will play in life, as the wife of my super-man. The union of a super-male with a highly gifted normal female is sure to result in—'

Mansfield caught his bony arm.

'You're going to do that!' he cried. 'This girl – that monster! You're going to mate them – like cattle?'

The scientist stared at him, surprised.

'What is wrong with that?' he squeaked. 'That has been my great dream – my lifelong ambition, which the world has laughed at! You, Mansfield, have never laughed at me. I like you. You alone, even though you are not a scientist, have been tolerant, understanding. That is why I have brought you here, why I have shown you the astounding secret which I have hidden from the world. Mansfield, I am going to create a new race of beings – a super-race of mankind! Mansfield, the race of normal humans is doomed – the world is doomed – the world which has laughed at me and scorned me as a fool! You, Mansfield, shall not be destroyed. I have brought you here to show you, to instruct you. I am sparing your life, Mansfield!'

The artist stared at the grotesque face before him. The man was mad, he felt sure, now. His eyes blazed with hate, his wizened features were distorted with a lusting for revenge. He seemed more inhuman than the giant he had brought to life in the test tube. Mansfield felt his flesh crawling with horror; but apparently the scientist did not observe his reaction.

'The World is ruled by dictators,' Thorndile went on passionately. 'Luccini, the master of United Europe – Sin Tao, the master-mind of the Oriental League – Channing, the President of the Federated North and South Americas. Super-men, the silly masses call *them*. Super-men, Mansfield! Ha, I'll show them! They shall all be destroyed. There will be one world dictator, one super-man. You have seen him. In a few moments you will talk with him. He will rule all beings on this planet, my friend, and from his loins will spring a new race, a super-race which shall hold such humans as are permitted to live in subjection, as slaves!'

With an effort, Mansfield got a grip on himself. He decided to humour the old professor. The thing he was talking about was absurd. Destroy the nations of the earth, except for a handful of slaves; create a new race! Why, the idea was preposterous – lunacy!

And yet – He glanced back at the test tube containing the lovely young woman. Thorndile had done this. Using his great knowledge of the very latest developments in many branches of ultra-modern science, he had accomplished a seeming miracle. If he could do the thing which other scientists had deemed impossible – if he had created a new scientific Adam and Eve – why not the rest?

'How, Professor, will you proceed to set up this super-man as world dictator?' he asked, trying to make his voice sound natural. 'What of the armies, the forces on land and sea and in the air? It seems to me an impossible undertaking!'

The scientist tapped Mansfield's chest with a bony finger.

'You are talking nonsense!' he scoffed. 'Armies, navies, airplanes! Of what use will they be against my super-man? Bullets will not harm him; poison gas will not kill him, any more than it can kill certain bacteria with which he is inoculated. The fellow is invulnerable, and I estimate his life-span at two hundred years!'

'Two hundred years!'

'Certainly! Now, listen to me, Mansfield. You have observed grasshoppers, have you not?'

'Grasshoppers? Certainly!'

'You have seen them leap great distances. A man who could catapult himself a corresponding distance for his size would be killed by the fall, would he not? Furthermore, a normal man would jerk his own legs off if he could spring from the ground with enough force to equal the grasshopper's feat, for his size. Or think of an enormous house fly, the size of a man. Think what a monster he would be, Mansfield – his strength, his relative invulnerability! Think of any insect, the ant, for instance. How does it compare with man, considering the difference in size between them?'

Mansfield wore a puzzled frown.

'What are you getting at, Thorndile?' he asked.

'Just this! Years ago I discovered how the flesh and blood and bones of a human infant could be treated in the embryonic stages so as to develop the best characteristics of insect life, yet leaving the brain all its highest functions of thought, will power and imagination. In fact, in the case of my super-man, I have been able, by the means of gland secretions, to give him a gigantic brain and a mind that transcends even my own ability to realize its powers!'

Mansfield shook his head slowly.

'All this sounds incredible,' he said, 'yet I am forced to believe you know what you are talking about. If I hadn't seen with my own eyes—' He paused, glancing at the sleeping beauty. 'What of her?' he asked, with a slight choke in his voice. She seemed so sweetly innocent that it pained the young artist to regard her as being in any way connected with all this scientific madness. 'Is she, too, invulnerable to ordinary death-dealing instruments?'

Thorndile jerked his egg-like head decisively. 'No,' he sneered, 'I have little interest in her, Mansfield. As soon as she has served my purpose she will be destroyed.'

'Destroyed!' Mansfield drew back.

The scientist cackled with amusement. 'Ha, your artistic sense is shocked at the idea of destroying such beauty!' he laughed. 'But it will be quite necessary to kill her, Mansfield. You see, my super-man must not be allowed to form any silly affection for her. It would seriously interfere with the future which I have so carefully mapped out for him. No, she is only a woman. I need her only that a new creature may be created, in my test tube. It will be, in a way, her child; but it will be a super-human, like its father. I shall make it a woman. As you know, science has discovered the origin of sex, though I am the first scientist to achieve a method of positive control. You see, the oocytes from which ova develop, and the spermatogonia which becomes sperms—'

A tremendous crash drowned out his shrill voice. Mansfield jumped. He heard the sound of falling glass, then an inhuman roar.

'What was that?' he cried.

The scientist's gaunt face had turned ashen; his eyes bulged.

'The glassite – the test tube!' he shrieked. 'He has broken out through a wall of solid glassite! Quick, Mansfield – *the super-man has been born!*'

CHAPTER III

THE MONSTER TAKES CHARGE

Mansfield, his legs stiff with horror, followed the running professor. Arriving at the smashed test tube he halted, staring in mingled artist admiration and human dread and antipathy at the towering, dripping giant that confronted the scientist and himself.

The naked super-man was even taller than he had appeared to be while in the test tube. Wet black hair clung to his huge head, but he was beardless and his elephantine torso was smooth and hairless. A silver valve at his navel took the place of a button. His muscles, still bearing the imprint of suction cups, rippled beneath thick ivory skin, as he took a step toward them.

Instinctively, Mansfield drew back. He was not by nature a timid person, yet the sight of this giant chilled his spine. But Thorndile, far from being afraid, appeared delighted with the spawn of his weird brain. Without further hesitation, he approached his offspring in an affectionate manner, and they stood together, the wizened old scientist and the super-man, like pigmy and elephantine Goliath, regarding each other.

'Ha, you decided to come out!' said the scientist. 'You should have waited. You have ruined a very expensive apparatus. I should not have forgotten. In my conversation with Mansfield, the time for your birth slipped by unnoticed. But you should have waited – you might have injured your knuckles on the glassite!'

The super-man writhed his face into a terrible scowl that seemed to frighten even the professor.

'I wait for no man!' he boomed, in a voice like thunder.

'But I am your master,' squeaked the scientist. 'I created you. You must obey me!'

The giant stretched out one long arm and caught Thorndile by his skinny neck. With the ease with which a cat tosses a helpless mouse into the air, he lifted the professor above his head. The old man's shriek was cut off by the big thumb on his throat; his legs kicked and dangled, and he tried weakly to tear the giant hand from his neck. Suddenly the super-man opened his hand, and the scientist dropped some ten feet to the floor.

'You, my master – *you!*' the super-man sneered. Then

he threw back his head and laughed so loud that Mansfield was almost deafened. The scientist recovered himself enough to get to his feet, where he stood swaying. Mansfield supported him.

'There is nothing you can teach me,' asserted the giant proudly. 'I have been in communication with your brain for over two years. How do I know how to speak? I have learned it telepathically. You are only a mortal – I am a super-man. Of what possible use can you be to me? Your mental processes are childish in comparison with mine. I know the plans you have made for me. Your mind has taught me everything; you do not need to tell me. I have *felt* the impressions of your thoughts, of your emotions. Tell me, you weakling, what good *can* you do me?'

'I – I—' quavered the professor, and stopped. He couldn't think of anything to suggest! 'But you can't kill *me*!' he protested. 'Common decency – a man's loyalty to his creator, his own father—'

'Are you trying to insult me.' thundered the monster, advancing threateningly.

Mansfield turned to flee, and the professor did likewise; but the super-man seemed only to find amusement in their terror.

'Mice!' he sneered, then chuckled. 'I'm going to have a lot of fun with you while I let you live. I have one thing which you never gave me, Thorndile – a sense of humour. That's a human trait I must have inherited from my human ancestors. But your talk of loyalty is nonsense, Thorndile! You have instilled only hate and malice in my impressionable mind; it's too late to change now. I'm what I am. You made me this way – it's only right for you to reap your reward.'

The scientist was speechless; he seemed paralyzed with fear.

'I am reading your minds right now,' the super-man asserted, his face expanding in a wolfish grin. 'You, Thorndile, are trying feverishly to think of some way to control my actions – it has even flashed into your contemptible mind to try to destroy me. But—' He chuckled with satisfaction. 'But you can't think of anything that could kill me!' he laughed.

'And you, Mansfield, are wondering about that girl – what I'm going to do with her. Well, you'll soon find out. Thorndile, I have absorbed most of your psychology, but there's one point on which I do not agree with you. I want that girl, Thorndile, and I'm going to have her. And that reminds me, I'd better take a look at her; I've only received the false impressions of your warped, woman-hating brain to tell me what she's like!'

He advanced with great strides, and the two men flung themselves desperately out of his path. He ignored them and went straight to the test tube containing the sleeping golden-haired girl.

Mansfield picked himself up from the floor and stared after the naked giant. Anger surged up in him, displacing fear and caution.

'He's not going to touch her!' he gritted. 'That girl is – human! He's a monster. Thorndile – an inhuman monster! Thorndile – *I'm going to kill him!*'

CHAPTER IV

DEATH OF THE MAD SCIENTIST

Seizing a stout surgeon's scalpel of dura-steel, Mansfield crept along the floor toward the new-born monster.

'Come back!' hissed the professor. 'You can't harm him – he will kill you!'

But Mansfield went on, unheeding. He saw the superman bending his huge back and peering in at the slumbering girl; and he knew only one thought – he must annihilate the inhuman freak!

Apparently the monster's clairvoyant perceptions were momentarily suspended by his conscious mind. He was deeply engrossed in his study of the unborn beauty, and Mansfield crept up within seven or eight feet of him without attracting his attention. Mansfield realized then that despite his superhuman powers of mind the giant could scarcely receive impressions from all persons in the world at once; the result would be confusion and perplexity, chaos. There were limitations to the fellow's perceptive powers, then; and that discovery gave Mansfield encouragement.

Slowly, cautiously, he rose to his feet raised the knife to strike. The giant did not move. Mansfield brought the blade down with all the strength of his right arm.

The monster grunted, whirled around. Mansfield's arm was numb. The knife lay on the floor. The impact with the super-man's flesh had produced only a slight dent, as if his skin were the hide of a rhinoceros!

For one awful moment Mansfield had the feeling that he was facing certain death. The giant's black eyes blazed with fury; then, surprisingly, his gaze took in the scalpel on the floor, and he threw back his head and roared with laughter.

'You – you puny ant!' he bellowed. '*You* – tried to kill *me*!'

The creature's perverted sense of humour kept him laughing for a full minute, big drops of tears rolling down his great cheeks. Finally he ceased, and the thunderous echoes died away.

'But,' he said, wiping his eyes with a huge forefinger, 'even ants have courage. I like your courage, Mansfield. I shall show you a special favour.'

Mansfield held his breath; he could not speak.

'I'll let you choose your own manner of dying,' said the giant. He turned back to his inspection of the girl, quite as if he had not been interrupted.

Finally he grunted, and began to fumble at an air-tight door of the test tube; a moment later he flung it open. Mansfield watched him remove the mechanical connections from the girl's body, then pick her up in his huge arms, as if she were a tiny infant. Holding her by the ankles in one hand, he administered a sound slap, as a physician spanks a newly born babe to clear its lung passage and close the placental circulation artery.

The girl screamed – the cry of a woman, not an infant. Mansfield clenched his fists in helpless rage. Yet the giant seemed to know what he was about. He turned her right side up and set her on her feet. She swayed weakly, then got her balance. Her blue eyes were wide with wonder. She looked all around, bewildered.

'Ha,' said the super-man, imitating the expression used by the scientist, from whose consciousness he had learned his speech, 'you are not so bad. Thorndile gave me a wrong impression of you. Too bad you are not a super-woman. But my mentality is not limited to that runt's conceptions; I shall devise a way to improve you, make you a giant like me. Already I have a theory.'

She stared at him, wide-eyed, timorous, apprehensive.

Mansfield was so ravished by her appealing beauty that he almost forgot his dread of the monster.

She turned and regarded him silently. The look in her blue eyes melted his heart. Suddenly he cried out.

'I have it! I understand now! You are—'

The monster interrupted him.

'You are right,' he rumbled. 'Your inferior mind has hit upon the truth. Thorndile visited you at your studio while your mind was intensely active with your inspiration of a super-woman, a goddess. He carried away an unconscious impression of maidenly perfection which has been conveyed to the sub-conscious mind of this girl, influencing her development. You, not Thorndile, are the author of her pulchritude. Mansfield, I find it possible to be grateful to you. I shall let you live for an indefinite period. I shall put you temporarily to work as my slave.'

The girl spoke for the first time in her life, falteringly.

'Mansfield – Mansfield,' she repeated slowly, in a soft, musical voice. 'Graeme – *Graeme* Mansfield?'

'Yes,' whispered the artist. 'You can speak! And – and you know me already?'

'It – it seems to be in my mind – that name,' she said. 'I can hear the name – it is associated with beauty – lovely things!'

The super-man frowned horribly at her, then he withered Mansfield with a glance of jealous rage.

'When I have performed an operation on certain of your glands,' he informed the girl, 'you will not waste your thoughts on trivial ideas of art. You will be coldly intellectual, as I am, except for my sense of humour. While I appreciated your beauty, it is your mental possibilities and the attraction of the opposite sex that really matter to me. I will raise you above the normal limitations of ordinary mortals; you shall grow to be a giant, physically and mentally, for I need a super-woman companion.'

Mansfield shuddered. He tried to repress a thought; saw the monster turn upon him, grinning horribly.

'You are thinking of killing me – again!' he growled. The words were followed by another burst of roaring laughter. He broke off suddenly, gave a tremendous leap that carried him clear across the long laboratory.

Mansfield spun around, just in time to see him land beside the professor, who had opened the door and was trying to escape outside. The monster clutched him by the scruff of the neck and carried him back, arriving beside the wide-eyed girl and her amazed companion in two bounds.

'Now I will have some fun,' chuckled the giant.

He tossed the trembling scientist on the floor, where the old man cringed, whining piteously.

'Thorndile,' rumbled the super-man, 'I am going to kill you with your own device. As I told you, I am familiar with all your plans. Your cosmo-wave is designed to end the life of every human being responding to a certain vibration. You intended to raise your own physical vibration, and Mansfield's, to protect yourself, leaving the majority of humanity to die instantly from this ether-wave. Your idea is a good one. I shall employ the high-frequency vibrator to protect my mate and also Mansfield, for the time being. *I* shall not need that protection, having the vibration of certain bacteria. But you, Thorndile, shall perish by your own invention!'

'No, no!' quavered the scientist. 'Let me live – you need me – to assist you! There are many things which you still need to learn, consciously. You have inherited only instincts, like a chick that comes from the shell and instinctively crouches in the grass at the shadow of a hawk!'

'You compare me with a low form of life, a chick!' sneered the monster. 'Have I not demonstrated super-intelligence, super-physical prowess? A baby chick is not invulnerable. *I am!*'

Pride was in his rumbling, arrogant voice – the pride and self-esteem of his creator, Thorndile. The giant bent down and picked up the surgeon's scalpel, snapped the dura-steel between his thumb and fore-finger, opened his huge mouth and swallowed the broken instrument with one gulp!

'If you would wait for me to die,' he grinned at Mansfield, 'I should have to prolong your life to equal my own span – two hundred years!'

Having delivered this proud statement, he seemed to mellow a trifle with self-satisfaction. A look akin to condescension and scornful pity came over his face. He stooped and picked up the scientist, who squealed in terror.

'Shut up!' growled the test tube monster. 'I've decided not to torture you. I'll subject you to a painless death at once.' Before either of them could move out of his reach, he swooped up Mansfield and the dripping-wet maiden in his other arm and walked in three-yard strides to a far corner of the laboratory.

'It will soon be over,' he comforted the scientist. 'You said I should have a son's reverence toward you. I am therefore making this compromise. Thorndile, you may pull the lever that will bring about your own end!'

He set his victims down in front of a glass-metal machine. The old man's eyes were popping out in terror as he was forced to look at his own diabolical invention.

Mansfield felt sick with horror. In his imagination he could see millions upon millions of men, women and children sinking lifeless to the streets and the floors of their homes. He felt himself on the verge of insanity.

'No, no! *Thorndile!* You can't do this – it's fiendish, ghastly! You can't Thorndile, you *can't*!'

Beside him the girl stood looking from one to the other in innocent wonder.

'I don't – don't understand,' she complained, touching Mansfield's arm. 'Will people – like us – stop living?'

Mansfield's arm went around her. He nodded silently.

'Will we – will you, Graeme, and I stop living?' she pursued.

'Some day, if not now,' he told her hoarsely. 'But this – this is *murder*!'

The super-man threw him a scornful glance. 'What sentimental nonsense!' he scoffed. 'Here – you two – in here!'

He caught them up and shoved them inside a glassite cabinet. Mansfield tried to struggle, but it was like a kitten pitting its strength against an elephant. Before the giant locked them in, however, he had time to hear the professor shrieking at him.

'Mansfield! He is not invulnerable! There is one weakness – all animal life is sustained by—'

The door slammed shut, cutting off the professor's

frantic voice. With the girl clinging to him in instinctive fear, he stared through the glassite at the scene before them.

Enraged at the scientist's statement, evidently divining his thoughts, the monster jerked away from the door, which he had paused to lock. He reached the old man in a single bound, but not in time to prevent the downward blow of the fire-axe in the scientist's desperate grasp.

No sound penetrated the cabinet, but Mansfield saw a pane of ordinary glass break, saw the axe cut into the heart of the delicate mechanism of the cosmo-wave machine.

The giant caught up the mad scientist and promptly tore his head from his shoulders. Mansfield turned away feeling that he was about to faint. With a violent effort of will, he kept his senses. He looked down at the girl, whose head was against his chest. He was thankful she had not seen the thing he had just witnessed. She was so young, so devoid of earthly understanding! He shuddered at the thought of what the test tube monster intended to do to her – transform her into a female monster like himself!

He began to examine the complicated mechanism in the corner of the cabinet, wishing desperately that he had more scientific knowledge.

'This changes the vibrations of protoplasm,' he muttered. 'If it is adjustable, it could lower the vibrations of even ordinarily indestructible bacteria to the frequency of human vibrations. But to destroy him, I'd have to be able to repair the cosmo-wave generating machine, and—'

Suddenly he realized that he must not transmit his thoughts to the mind of his captor; so he began to think, over and over: 'I do *not* know how to kill him – I do *not* know how to kill him!' Yet in his sub-consciousness a half-formed idea had impressed itself.

At that moment the door opened and a mighty hand dragged him out.

'You are trying to conceal your treacherous thoughts from me, you miserable man-animal!' snarled the monster. 'Now I am going to kill you – just as you saw me kill Thorndile!'

Mansfield was hoisted above the giant's head so quickly that his senses reeled. Obviously, he was being poised preparatory to being dashed into lifeless pulp against the opposite wall.

A faint cry came from the girl. The monster lowered his victim a trifle to turn and look at her. She was lying insensible in the doorway. He carelessly dropped the artist and hastened to pick her up.

Mansfield tried to break his fall by twisting in mid-air and throwing out his arms, but he only partially succeeded. His head came into violent contact with the hard floor . . .

CHAPTER V

THE MONSTER EMPLOYS HYPNOTISM

Mansfield gained consciousness to find himself clasped in the arms of the girl. Disregarding his throbbing head, he struggled into an upright sitting posture; she was too inexperienced to restrain him.

'Graeme,' she whispered tenderly. 'You are – you live?'

He groaned, which brought to her beautiful face an expression of pity and slight perplexity.

'What happened?' he asked, looking around. He had been reclining in an arm chair in the late Professor Thorndile's library, the girl kneeling beside him and embracing him. 'I was afraid,' he muttered, 'that something had happened to you – that vibration instrument, or something—'

'I was faint with hunger,' she said soberly. 'The man

giant sent for food, which men brought. The men ran away, frightened. We both ate, and now I am well.'

Mansfield jumped to his feet, swaying as the blood left his head; then his faintness passed away and he went to the single door of the library. It was unlocked.

'Where's that monster?' he asked the girl.

'He is repairing the killing machine,' she said. 'He said he is soon to make himself world dictator. I do not understand, even yet, Graeme.'

Mansfield turned toward the windows without replying.

'We've got to get out of here,' he whispered hurriedly. 'We can't leave by the door, for then we'd have to go through the laboratory, where he would catch us. Come, we'll climb down from this window and escape! Here, wear this!'

He snatched up a robe from the arm chair and draped it hastily over her shoulders. 'Some people are still opposed to nudism,' he explained. 'We'll get you some clothes. My, how beautiful you are – Daphne!'

'Daphne?' she echoed.

'Yes, I'm going to call you Daphne. Tell you the story some day, about the lovely nymph Daphne. But come – we must hurry!'

Opening the window nearest him, he caught her up and was just helping her over the sill when he heard a step outside the door. He leaped toward the door, locked it, then dashed back to the window.

There was a fearful crash, and the door was torn from its hinges. The super-man, ducking his head to pass through the doorway, reached the pair in a flying bound, caught one in either hand, and jerked them back into the room.

'So you thought you could escape!' he growled.

The monster was fully clothed, in a well-cut suit that did justice to his marvellous physique. Despite his disappointment, Mansfield felt an artist's appreciation of his splendid figure.

The giant, seeming to read his thoughts, looked down

at himself and smiled with self-satisfaction. Evidently his pleasure at his victim's admiration had temporarily allayed his wrath.

'You are wondering,' he rumbled, 'how I procured these garments. I will satisfy your curiosity, Mansfield. Thorndile had these clothes made for me some weeks ago. He was not considerate enough of his other experiment to provide her with attire. That is because he intended to destroy her presently.'

Mansfield started to open his mouth to speak.

'Now you are wishing to ask why I have spared your life, what I intend to do with you. The first part of that question I will answer. You will be of momentary use to me, Mansfield. My size alarms people, so I am going to send you out with the girl you have presumed to call Daphne to purchase suitable clothing for her.'

Here he burst into uproarious laughter.

'You think you see a way to escape me!' he said, when he had controlled his humour enough to speak. 'Mansfield, is there no limit to human folly? You should know that what you are thinking is silly. Come here, Mansfield!'

The artist recoiled from his super-human master in revulsion. The monster's black eyes were fastened on his in a penetrating gaze; he felt his mind going blank, as if he were going under a spell. *Hypnotism!* The word flashed upon his weakening consciousness.

'Graeme! Graeme!' called the girl. Her voice sounded faint, distant, fearful. 'Don't sleep, Graeme! I need you, Graeme!'

Tearing his gaze from the monster's terrible eyes, Mansfield sought to hold on to consciousness.

'You can't hypnotize me!' he gritted, surprised that his own voice seemed so far off. 'Only a willing subject, or one paralyzed by fear, can be hypnotized!'

'And you,' mocked the super-man, 'are utterly afraid of me! Mansfield, you are partially hypnotized at this moment. You can still act independently to some extent, which will enable you to carry out my orders in a natural manner; but you are powerless to withstand my will, Mansfield. See! I beckon. Come here, Mansfield!'

At the sound of that booming command, Mansfield found himself obeying. He went straight toward the monster, surprised at his own action, but unable to conceive an impulse to disobey. He knew that he was under mild hypnosis, yet it didn't seem to matter.

The super-man opened a drawer in the dead scientist's desk, held out a pistol. 'Here, Mansfield,' he said. 'Shoot!'

Without knowing why he did it, Mansfield took the weapon, turned and levelled it at the wide-eyed girl.

'Awaken, Mansfield!' commanded the giant hypnotist.

Mansfield blinked his eyes, stared at Daphne in horror; the weapon slipped from his nerveless fingers.

'Daphne!' he cried. 'I was about to kill you!'

Thunderous laughter drowned out his voice, made the walls vibrate. 'Ho-ho-ho!' roared the monster. 'How white you are, Mansfield! Ho-ho-ho! Now do you think you can disobey me?'

Suddenly he sobered. 'You will do what I tell you,' he said. 'I shall work on the cosmo-wave generator. I am having difficulty with it, because that fool scientist left no spare parts. Yet I shall devise means. My intelligence is superior to that of any man living. Meanwhile, you will take my Daphne – I find that name as good as any other – to the best shops and purchase clothes for her. Look at me, Mansfield. You will return here in exactly one hour, do you hear? *Look at me, I said!*'

But Mansfield was not looking at him; with all the power of his conscious mind he was concentrating on the weapon on the floor. He wanted to pick it up, but he felt himself already going under the spell again, and it seemed strangely impossible to bend down and snatch up the gun.

'All right – pick it up,' said the giant, and Mansfield was suddenly able to reach down and grab the pistol.

He aimed it straight at the monster's heart, pressed the trigger. The roar that shattered the silence of the room was followed by a slight groan. The giant lay on the floor!

Then, to Mansfield's amazement and consternation, he got to his feet and towered over the artist. There was a small round hole in the monster's coat, but he seemed to have recovered already. He opened his shirt and revealed a pink spot where the bullet had flattened itself against his skin.

'I have not yet gotten my full strength,' he growled, 'or the bullet would not have had even that effect. In a day or two—' he frowned, listening. Mansfield listened, too, but heard nothing but his own breathing.

He watched while the giant stepped to the radiovision set and dialled in a station. Evidently his telepathic powers had divined something that was being broadcast. The vision-mirror showed a scrambled scene, which clarified as the giant brought the station in more clearly. Mansfield saw a scene at the airport. A man's voice was speaking.

'The attempted flight to Mars has been postponed,' the voice said. 'The rocket which you see is in readiness for the attempt, but at the last moment Professor Wingford has refused to fly it. This is a sad disappointment to us all, because there seems to be little doubt that the venture would be successful if an intelligent and fearless person could be found who would risk his life for the glory of science and our great nation! The Mars Expedition Committee has asked me to announce that any person wishing to volunteer for this great undertaking should communicate with them immediately. Every safeguard for the life of its occupant which modern science can provide is contained in the rocket-ship.

'As you all know, we have received recently what seem to be radio messages from the inhabitants of Mars. Our best linguists and code experts have not yet succeeded in interpreting these messages, but we have reason to believe that the Martians are aware of the projected flight to their planet, and that they wish to encourage the enterprise.

'It will be a great disappointment to them, no doubt, as well as to all Earthmen if this experiment ends in failure, owing to the unwillingness of scientifically trained men to volunteer to pilot the ship

'Somewhere within the sound of my voice such a person may exist. I urge such person or persons to get in touch with this station or the airport committee at once. There is no time to lose. The liquid air, which provides the cooling medium to offset atmospheric friction, has already been released in the walls of the ship—'

Frowning, but with a thoughtful gleam in his black eyes, the giant shut off the radio-vision set and the announcer's voice was stilled; the gigantic rocket-ship and the throng surrounding it soon vanished from the mirror.

'Fools!' scoffed the monster. 'Puny-minded idiots!'

'*You* are the person for that job!' cried Mansfield. 'You alone could succeed. Think of the admiration you would arouse, not only among men but among the Martians! You would be the greatest hero ever born! You would be made a *king* – ruler of two planets! You would—'

But the giant silenced him with a terrible look.

'I was born to destroy,' he said. 'I am what I am. It pleases me to wipe out the inhabitants of this earth, to institute a super-race of my own. Only a few thousand will survive the cosmo-wave, and they shall become my slaves. I need not leave this room, Mansfield, to subjugate the entire population of the earth. There are no physical limitations to the powers of my mind – I can influence the present rulers by simply projecting my will, and they will have to obey me, just as you do! I hold in my hands the destiny of every living being on this planet. Later, I myself will attend to Mars! The Martians, too, shall be destroyed!'

He turned and glared at Daphne.

'You are in love with this foolish artist!' he scowled. 'You hate me, as he does! Very well, I will waste no more time! I will alter your glands at once. When you need clothes, they will be large ones. And your lover I will kill. I shall find other slaves!'

The girl recoiled fearfully as he advanced in a single stride and lifted her roughly in his arms.

With the speed of a panther, Mansfield sprang forward, thrust the muzzle of the pistol in the monster's ear, and fired.

The giant fell on his face. Swiftly Mansfield fired into his ear again. The monster half rose, then fell forward.

Pulling the girl to her feet, Mansfield ran with her across the fallen door and through the laboratory to the street, still clutching the gun.

'I'm afraid he's not dead even yet!' he gasped. 'I heard him stirring!' As they ran, he recalled the scientist's dying words. If the monster still lived – if only cutting off his supply of oxygen could kill him—

'But who can overpower *that* fiend?' he thought. 'If glassite can't hold him, neither could a steel prison! It's a job for scientists, not an artist like me!'

He hailed an autoplane taxi.

'Come on, Daphne!' he gasped. 'We're going to volunteer to fly that rocket-ship! *We're going to Mars!*'

CHAPTER VI

A DESPERATE ATTEMPT

Most of the spectators had left the airport when they arrived, though a considerable crowd of curious, disappointed onlookers still surrounded the mighty, gleaming space-ship. Mansfield and Daphne pressed through and encountered a group of important-looking individuals who stood talking together. Their gloomy countenances brightened when Mansfield explained his business. Mansfield waved down their questions concerning his qualifications to pilot the ship and send back messages concerning the flight.

'I can manage it!' he shouted, glancing apprehensively over his shoulder. 'There is a giant – a monster – a super-man – I tried to kill him, but he may be alive yet. He will annihilate mankind unless he is somehow destroyed!'

One of the officials caught the eyes of the other. He tapped his forehead significantly; then smiled.

'I'm afraid we can't use you,' said one. 'You see—'

'Listen to me!' pleaded Mansfield. 'I'm not crazy! This monster was brought to being in a test tube. He is super-human. Professor Thorndile—'

'Ah!' cried a chorus of voices. '*Thorndile?*'

'Yes! He is dead! His own test tube monster killed him. He will kill you, too – all of us, unless—'

'*Thorndile's mysterious experiment!*' murmured one of the officials thoughtfully. 'A brilliant scientist, until a few years ago, when he announced that—'

'Quick!' yelled Mansfield. 'How do you operate this ship? I have warned you about Thorndile's monster – the rest is up to you gentlemen of science!' He helped Daphne climb up the ladder, entered the rocket-ship after her.

Hope, perplexity, consternation, doubt, fear – conflicting emotions were written in the scientists' faces. The leader suddenly decided to seize the opportunity afforded them by this lunatic. He nodded. The chief inventor mounted the ladder and showed Mansfield the most important details of the control mechanism.

'Full instructions are printed on this chart.' he said. He was looking regretfully at the beautiful girl beside the amateur pilot. 'Who is this young lady?' he asked. 'Must she join in this hazardous enterprise?'

A blood-curdling roar interrupted him.

Mansfield caught a glimpse of a giant grasshopper in human form soaring over the heads of the cringing, astonished spectators – straight toward the rocket-ship!

'Get out!' he yelled, touching the acceleration-button. The space-ship quivered, as gas escaped through the exhaust. While Mansfield fingered the control lever, trying frantically to remember what he had been told, the official tumbled out of the compartment, terrified at the thing he saw bounding toward them. Mansfield touched a second button in feverish hope, gave a cry of triumph as the ship's exhaust emitted a thunderous series of explosions that moved it slightly. He was getting the hang of it – this third button for the take-off, the rest to increase the speed—

He delayed the fraction of a second too long. With an ear-splitting bellow of mad rage, the monster leaped to the door of the rocket-ship, disdaining the ladder, and hauled the frightened girl outside. Mansfield, seeing the woman he loved torn from his side, did not press the take-off button. Life without Daphne—

Throwing open the door on the opposite side, he flung himself out in a wild effort to elude the menacing hands of the monster, who bounded back into the space-ship, murder blazing in his black eyes. But again he was too late. A giant hand caught his coat-tail as he fell; Mansfield dangled in mid-air.

The explosions of the exhaust suddenly became a mighty roar – the rocket-ship shot skyward!

Mansfield found himself on the ground. He heard the gasping cries of the throng, stood up and gaped, just in time to see a silver streak vanishing in the clear blue heavens.

No one else moved; no one could move. All eyes were turned upward in stupified amazement.

'He accidentally touched one of those buttons,' Mansfield muttered. 'That sent the ship off – ripped my coat. Is his hand caught in the door, held by wind-pressure? But no – he's practically beyond our atmosphere by now, and—'

Daphne stumbled toward him; he took her in his arms.

'That monster won't menace you any more,' he consoled her. 'He's on his way to another planet!'

'I'm glad, Graeme – glad!' cried the girl, clinging to him.

'So am I, sweet,' he agreed. 'Now I can make you my wife. Yes, I'm mighty glad, but—'

He grinned at the officials, who had gathered their wits and were coming forward to ply him with the questions that trembled on their lips.

'—but I sure feel sorry for the people on Mars!' Mansfield said.

The Golden Amazon Returns

by John Russell Fearn

'Four years,' mused Chris Wilson. 'Four years of comparative peace and quiet. It's almost unbelievable.'

He stretched out his lithe body more comfortably in the soft, flaming verdure that formed the entire makeup of this part of the Hotlands of Venus. Lazily his gaze travelled over the quiet clearing, past the cumbersome but friendly monstrosities of the Hotlanders browsing in the heat; then finally to his young goddess of a wife – the former Violet Ray – stretched beside him.

'Yes, four years,' she agreed. 'I've nearly forgotten how to use my muscles . . . The name "Golden Amazon" is getting little better than a legend. Instead I'm a mother and darn near a domesticated wife. Yet . . . I like it.'

Chris smiled, and allowed his thoughts to travel back to the time when he had first learned of the legendary 'Golden Amazon'. The only survivor of a space wreck on Venus, she had been found as a baby by Venusian Hotlanders. They had taken care of her, and the child had matured in the environment of Venus, where cosmic rays were blocked by the succeeding layers of atmosphere, but where solar radiations, due to the planet's proximity to the sun, seeped through. The outcome was steady anabolism, which transformed her into a woman utterly unlike any other. Instead of human cells breaking down, they had built up to ever increasing toughness. Her intelligence had matched her physique, and she had been able to educate herself from records of old books and tapes which remained inside the space ship that had fallen to Venus. The girl had developed into a lone wolf, dedicated to smashing the criminal elements which had caused the spaceship to crash, killing her parents along with the rest of the crew. As a result of becoming embroiled in her fight, Chris had married her.

The Amazon's deep blue eyes moved to two tiny forms lying in the vegetation close by – a boy and a girl, twins, every part of their exposed skin as golden yellow as their mother's.

'Some day,' she went on slowly, 'those two children of ours are going to grow up, Chris – form the nucleus of a new species. Twenty-five years ago an accident dropped me on this planet and made me a superwoman. That strength, that inborn knowledge of the Venusian jungle and the wilds of space, has been handed on to them. My strength; your civilized culture – Grand combination!'

'Hercules and Hygeia,' Chris reflected. 'God of strength and goddess of health – Yep, we chose good names for them – but I still like "The Heavenly Twins" better . . .'

Vi relaxed again, pondered. 'Wonder what ever became of Welgand?' she muttered. 'Remember how we got all that gang of crooks, but he just faded away into space? And been gone these four years – Not like him to do that. Of course he's all washed up so far as establishing a criminal domination of Earth is concerned, but it's surprising he's made no effort to get at you and me. Seems logical he would want to break us since we broke him.'*

'Let him try!' Chris said grimly; then he shrugged. 'Oh be damned to him! We've made our home here; we're happy and comfortable. Why should we bother about—?'

He broke off and sat up suddenly, frowning, as an unaccustomed sound broke the sweltering silences of the jungle. It was the recognizable throb of a space ship's underjets.

'That's odd!' he ejaculated. 'Who'd want to come over these Hotlands anyway?'

*'The Amazon Fights Again' – *Fantastic Adventures*, June 1940.

Vi jumped to her feet, hand shading her eyes. The Hotlanders were now starting to shift about uneasily, moving into the shelter of the jungle as though in anticipation of some danger.

'Something wrong here,' the girl said briefly. 'The Hotlanders can sense it quicker than we can – Yes, look!' she finished with a cry; and at that identical moment a small but powerful spaceship, its underjets now cut off, came gliding into view at low altitude over the drooping verdure of the trees. It moved unerringly towards the little clearing.

Abruptly Chris was alive to the danger. He saw a lens uncover in the base of the ship and at the same instant a blue beam cut through the hot and dusty air. It blasted a cindery scorching trail straight along to where the girl stood. Paralyzed with amazement she stared at it; then with a mighty leap Chris dived, shoved her, sent both of them staggering into the undergrowth.

'What goes on?' Vi panted, wheeling round. 'Who *is* it anyway? Unless it's—'

She broke off, watching tensely as the little ship circled abruptly, swept back again with raygun blazing dangerously. Then from the vessel's side there suddenly dropped a life-anchor.* Down it fell, stopped within inches of the two sleeping infants in the vegetation. Just as quickly it recoiled, swept the two into the air, and they vanished in the open lock. Then with a burst of aggressive fire the ship nosed upward, headed voidward with ever increasing speed.

For a full five seconds Vi was too stunned to speak. Then Chris mumbled dazedly, 'A snatch! They stole the kids and—'

'Welgand!' Vi clenched her fists. 'Just as we were talking about him, too. Somehow he got to know of our hideout and – Come on!'

*Life anchor – so called because it attracts living tissue as an ordinary magnet attracts steel. – Ed.

Chris followed her hurriedly across the clearing, into the jungle where their spaceship *Ultra* lay parked.

'Say, we don't know where he's heading,' Chris pointed out.

'We'll find out!' Vi retorted. 'Space is a big place, and if you think I'm lying around while he steals my babies you're mistaken. Get in!'

'But wait a minute, Vi! That was an obvious snatch. It may have been a trick to—'

The girl listened to no more. With one thrust of her whipcord arm she bundled Chris through the airlock, slammed it shut, then hurried across to the control board.

'Trouble with you, Chris . . .' she manoeuvred the superfast little machine over the treetops into the densely misted sky, 'is that you talk first and act afterward. That isn't jungle law. If that *is* Welgand' – her jaws tightened – 'I'll finish the job I once nearly accomplished! And if he harms either of our babies God help him!'

Chris nodded grimly; he knew she meant it. Then he looked out of the port. In a few minutes he picked up the distant fast travelling space machine which had made the lightning abduction.

'Don't recognize it as an ordinary vessel,' he commented. 'No planetary insignia or anything – Of course a wanted criminal would hardly use a ship anybody could recognize—'

'Hardly!' Vi stared through her own window. 'So he's heading Moonward. Wonder what he wants there?'

With that she slammed on the power to maximum, lay back with straining muscles as the frightful acceleration all but crushed the breath out of her. Chris sat down with a thud, gulping for breath. These dizzying dives through space, painful even for the superhuman girl, always left him shaken and sweating.

'Sorry – got to do it,' she said curtly. 'This is business – grim business. Lie down while we go to it . . .'

Chris obeyed weakly, and from then on the girl kept

the ship on full power except for intervals when sheer physical anguish and the need for food demanded a relinquishment. Even so, the distant space machine managed to keep its flying start.

And to Vi's mounting fury the distance did not lessen between them.

Through the hours – grinding hours; through Earth days – and still the bridge was not closed. Evidently the abductor was using a highly volatile mixture in his rocket chambers.

It became clear though as the time passed that the goal was the moon. Its Earth-illuminated mass – for it was almost at new Moon – became larger and larger, until at last the little ship was a silvery speck in the sunshine silhouetted against the copper bowl of the Moon.

'Vi, I still think there is more behind this than a plain snatch,' Chris insisted, watching intently through the glass. 'If you weren't so volcanic in your methods we'd have time to reason it out—'

'Yeah, and he'd have time to kill my babies! Welgand wouldn't stop at that, don't you forget it!' Vi stopped, her eyes narrowed as she peered ahead. Sunshine had left the distant ship now but it was still just possible to follow its movements. 'Tycho crater, eh? That's where he's making for. Better get the spacesuits ready.'

Chris did so and she still watched intently. Finally she looked through the telescopic mirror and saw the ship land on the wide, sprawling crater of Tycho. Dimly she could see the mystic streaks and rays from the crater in the Earthshine. It made it difficult to see what happened to the ship – but apparently it vanished at last in a crack.

Vi straightened up from the mirror, face grim.

'He's gone inside the Moon,' she said. 'Take over while I get a suit on.'

Chris nodded; then when she was ready, barring helmet, he did likewise. With practised hands the girl brought the little ship down into the inky shadows of the range round the vast Tycho crater, closed the anchor switches, then screwed on her helmet and snapped on the intercommunication.

'Whatever happens, we stick together,' she announced. 'It may be a trick, even as you figured, but either way we'll beat it. Come on.'

She slapped a raygun belt around her waist then opened the airlock. She paused, surprised. Chris too halted. Now they came to look at Tycho's floor at close quarters, most of it quite clear in the Earthshine, they saw there was something queer about it. It radiated streaks and rays as usual in hazy pearl-like lustre, only it was *not* a rocky arid plain . . .

'Say, this is – glass!' Vi murmured. 'Or something very like it!'

She was right. The fact became clearer as they advanced out onto it. It stretched perhaps a mile in diameter and then merged into the rocky foothills of the spiked mountains surrounding the crater.

'Not glass, but a mineral of some kind,' the girl said, her face perplexed inside her helmet. 'Wonder what— ? Oh, be hanged! We've a job to do. We've got to find that crack— Over there, I think.'

They started on a hurried, earnest search. It ended at last in a distinctly visible cleft leading downwards in the foothills.

'Yes, this must be it,' Chris decided, gazing down. 'A spaceship could get down if skilfully driven. We go below?'

Vi didn't trouble to answer that. She swung herself lithely in the trifling gravitation and began to scramble down into the depths. Utter darkness closed round the pair of them – the complete abysmal dark of lunar night. Then as she descended Vi felt something scraping its way up her body. She had gone below it before she had realized it was a sprung trapdoor opened by the pressure of her body. Chris' feet became visible through it as she switched on her helmet-lamp. Then as they both came below the trap it sprang shut again—

A voice spoke curtly, suddenly. It was a grim merciless voice that neither of them had heard for four years.

'Okay, take your helmets off! There's air down here!'

Slowly Vi turned, realized she was now on flat ground, inside an immense underground cave. Lights came up suddenly from roughly slung electric globes. A little distance away across the enormous space was the ship they had been pursuing. Immediately facing her and Chris was a tall man in flying kit, thin-faced, black haired, sunken-cheeked.

'Welgand!' Vi eyed him for a moment, unscrewed her helmet and shook free her jet black hair. 'I guessed it—'

'Still smart, eh, Amazon?' he asked dryly. 'And still spoiling for a fight! I figured on that. That's why I frisked those brats of yours. Took me some time to locate your hideout, but I made it at last—'

'Where are they?' Vi broke in venomously. 'If you've hurt them in the slightest, Welgand, I'll—'

'Hurt them?' Welgand grinned crookedly. 'I've killed them! That makes you squirm, doesn't it? Killed 'em, I tell you, just as I'll kill you next and this nosey husband of yours! Why did I snatch the brats anyway? Because I figured you'd come blundering after 'em – *Here* where nobody can help you, where no Hotlanders or Venusian jungles can be your allies. Smart, eh?'

Vi hardly heard the most of Welgand's words. 'I've killed them!' was the one thing blazing through her brain; and when it registered in its full murderous implication she sprang forward almost involuntarily, gloved hands outflung. With bone-cracking force her fingers closed over Welgand's raygun hand – But in the interval of years he had evidently learned a trick or two.

He bent his knees suddenly, relaxed, then twisted.

Vi found herself flung clean over his head; but she fell lightly in the slight gravity and in that time Chris had thrown himself into the attack. He managed to land a slogging punch that sent Welgand reeling, but he still held onto his gun.

Then as Vi scrambled to her feet and prepared to leap again she stopped, relaxed. The big underground place had suddenly become alive with men. A dozen at least, all with guns steadily pointed.

'Better take it easy,' Welgand advised harshly, straightening up. 'Get those spacesuits off, the pair of you. Al, take their guns!'

CHAPTER II

SOLAR VENGEANCE

When the job of frisking had been done Chris and the girl stood passive. But there was a mask of vindictive fury on Vi's face that reminded Welgand of a tigress robbed of her cubs. He tightened his hold on his gun, jerked his head.

'Get moving!'

Outnumbered, boiling with fury, Chris and Vi obeyed. They crossed the waste of cavern then through a naturally chiselled hole in the rock face. It brought them into an even mightier place. Over their heads at a considerable height was a grey mineral roof, supported on four titanic pillars of pumice rock. In the floor of the cavern, contrived so as to be exactly centred under the mineral roof, was a pit. It was perhaps half a mile across and apparently went down into nothing.

Vi turned from looking into the inexplicable depths.

'Well, get on with it!' she snapped. 'Going to throw us down there, I suppose? What are we waiting for?'

Welgand came up with a grim smile. 'You underrate

me, Amazon,' he murmured. 'Throwing you down there is not my object, even though it does go right through to a lens on the Moon's other side. It's really quite a clever device, I flatter myself. There are shields controlled from my power-room—'

Vi looked puzzled. 'Lens? Right through the Moon?'

'I assure you I have not been idle in these four years – Keep on moving, both of you – up those stone steps there.'

Bullied by the guns they moved up the steps indicated and found themselves rising to the level of the mineral roof. A trapdoor in the wall let them through on to the top of it. It was the floor now, not the ceiling – but above was yet another roof of natural mineral.

'Just what is this?' Chris demanded, swinging round. 'What's the idea of this glorified ballroom floor business—?'

'Did you notice the centre of Tycho's crater floor?' Welgand asked.

'Yeah, sure – Mineral, polished, like frosted glass—' Chris gave a start. 'You mean this is it?'

'Above your heads there – the roof,' Welgand said. 'In all, there are three mineral sections like that here – and a similar set up on the Moon's other side. The mineral is quartz isotope, peculiar to the Moon. I have had them ground into special shapes, these sections. I believe the Moon's streaks and rays are explained by the quartz. I used big proportions of it to make giant lenses. Every condenser lens has three parts, as you know. Below you – this floor – is one lens. Affixed to it and forming the roof of the cavern we just left is the second lens; above in the floor of Tycho is the third lens. A complete giant condenser. And on the other side of the Moon is an identical setup.'

'But – but what—?' Chris gazed mystifiedly at the girl.

Welgand gave a grim smile and snapped his fingers. Two of his trigger men came in with immensely strong metal frameworks, perhaps six feet high, and supplied with heavy triple linked chain.

'Fasten 'em up!' he ordered briefly; then watched as Vi and Chris were forced into the frames, their wrists drawn up to the diagonal corners, their ankles likewise. The manacles clicked, left them both spreadeagled with feet barely on the frame bottom.

'This time,' Welgand said steadily, putting his gun away, 'I am going to do the thing properly, Amazon – same to you, Wilson. I had those frames made specially of hardened triple-x steel, proof against even your muscles, I guess.'

'Suppose you quit drivelling and tell us what the idea is?' Vi suggested bitterly.

'Okay.' Welgand's thin face darkened. 'Because of you, Amazon, my schemes for the domination of the world collapsed: I was forced to dash into space as a fugitive. Only one thing was left for me – revenge! Revenge on you and the Earth which outlawed me! For four years I have worked on this scheme, gathered a few men around me – fugitive engineers and suchlike. To cut it short, we decided to use the natural quartz of the Moon for a giant lens. We bored a tunnel right through the Moon, a tunnel specially arranged to dead centre on this giant lens. It was not difficult because the Moon is honeycombed with pumice rock anyway. When the shields in the tunnel are withdrawn – actuated by my power house machinery – the sun when at the zenith on the other side of the Moon – that is new Moon to Earth – shines right down the tunnel as a single ray and passes through these lenses.'

'Well?' Chris said that, uncomprehending. But the girl's face was becoming strained as she glimpsed the underlying idea.

'Tomorrow – that is in two hours – it will be absolute new moon,' Welgand said slowly. 'And tomorrow is the twentieth of February, 2064. There is a total eclipse of the sun on the Earth. So, when I withdraw my shields—'

'A cosmic burning glass!' Vi cried in horror, suddenly getting at the truth. 'A ray of concentrated solar power and heat burning through the moon, gathered into focus by these lenses and—'

'And concentrated on Earth, since this side of the Moon obviously faces the Earth at all times.' Welgand gave a merciless grin. 'Revenge! The mightiest revenge one man ever took – ! A ray, sweeping at two thousand miles an hour across the world! First Alaska, across the Pacific, across the United States – to Europe – Yes, across the most populated parts of the world. And deep in the umbra's absolute cone shadow will lie death! A burning trail will be left everywhere the total eclipse passes, just as a sunlight recording globe leaves a charred trail along its chart. Magnificent, is it not?'

'You're mad!' Chris shouted desperately, struggling futilely to tear himself loose from the chains. 'You can't do this thing, Welgand—'

'I'm not mad, just ingenious,' he said softly. 'And . . . embittered. I have arranged it so that you will be the first to feel the shaft of unthinkable heat as it blasts up the tunnel to these lenses. Being between the lenses you will char to cinders. A few seconds later when the beam hits Earth others will die – Those damnable, stinking others who outlawed me! Total eclipse is right. Now you know why I brought you here.'

Welgand stopped, turned away sharply to the metal trapdoor in the wall, slammed and bolted it behind him. The two were alone in the dim yellow light of a single power bulb. And that bulb – clever thought! – was placed directly over an electric clock. It clicked steadily as it chopped off half seconds.

'A fiend!' Chris whispered. 'That's what he's become, Vi – No longer a master scientist with a criminal brain, but a monster! First he kills our kids, chains us up like this, then – Do you realize hundreds of the Earth's best scientists will be watching the eclipse and will get the full blast of the ray? Moving at two thousand miles an hour there'll be hardly a chance to get clear of it—!'

'That obviously is part of the inhuman ingenuity of the idea,' Vi said slowly. 'Only thing I do not believe is that he killed the babies: that was put in to torture us. He's got more sense than destroy children with such possibilities—' She came suddenly to action. 'Somehow we've got to move! We've *got* to! Everything depends on it—'

With that she looked up and studied her wrists drawn diagonally up over her head. She pulled with all her strength on the chains, but Welgand had been right. They were proof against her muscles this time. And again, the frames were so designed as to make any real effort impossible. Time and again Vi threw herself into the effort, but without success. Her feet hardly touched the frame bottom anyway.

'No dice?' Chris asked hollowly.

'Nope. Seems Welgand has— Wait a minute!' A gleam came into the girl's eyes. 'There may be one trick he forgot – the lesser gravity! It's worth a try.'

Puzzled, Chris watched her. She lurched herself back and forth violently until the entire frame toppled over, slamming her spreadeagled on her back.

'What's the good of that?' Chris demanded, staring down as he saw her gathering her supple body for a tremendous effort.

'Just this— Pulling downwards against my wrists *towards* gravity, and with my feet nearly clear of the ground, was useless. But lying flat and tugging horizontally I've got the gravity as my advantage. I've got about three times the normal pulling power which should compensate for the extra thickness of chain – Here we go!'

Chris watched with bated breath as she suddenly threw everything she had got into the muscles of her arms. It was an amazing sight as she dragged on the frame like one racked. Harder – harder, until the tendons and veins stood out on her arms and shoulders, until her face began to flush with the strain.

Then came that sound Chris had so often heard before – the creaking, crunching grind of metal parting along its forged ends. Again! Vi was like a stretched spring – *Again!* And the chains holding her wrists snapped abruptly. She relaxed instantly, breathing hard.

After a moment or two she was herself again, sat up and wrenched at the chains on her ankles. They gave way at last and she stood up, manacles still on her wrists and legs. She gave a ghostly smile.

'Chains do not a prison make,' she misquoted. 'Now let's see what we can do with you . . .'

It was easier with Chris for their combined efforts went to work. In a few minutes he was free, stood up beside the girl as she massaged her grazed and bleeding wrists.

'Now for Welgand,' Chris breathed ominously, staring round the grey expanse.

They hurried to the metal door. That it was locked they had fully expected since they'd heard Welgand slam the bolts. The girl pulled at it, shook her head, thought. Then her eyes wandered to the ticking electric clock.

'Yes, it's a chance,' she murmured. 'Put that clock out of action and a fuse will blow somewhere in Welgand's powerhouse. He'll be sure to investigate – or send somebody to do it. Part of the essential torture, don't forget. Right! Stand by that door. Moment somebody comes in shut it and leave the rest to me.'

She turned, gave a mighty leap against the weak gravity. It carried her up momentarily to the clock. She drove her fist right into its face to the accompaniment of a blinding flash, then dropped back to the lens floor. In a moment she was at the door opposite Chris, her body quivering expectantly.

Her hunch had been right for presently there came

sounds outside the door. Bolts slammed; the door opened. Two trigger men came straight in with levelled guns. The moment they saw the fallen, empty frames they stopped and stared.

'What in hell—?' one of them started to say; then he broke off with a gurgling grunt as a yellow arm hooked out of the gloom and crushed under his bristly chin. His companion was no better off, for as he turned an arm hooked under his jaw too.

Turning ever so slightly both men could see the face of the girl between their own. It was wearing an expression that struck horror deep into their souls.

'Take – take it easy, Amazon,' the one gasped, striving frantically to free himself. 'I've – I've nothing against you—'

'I've plenty against you though,' she breathed. 'No quarter this time! It's not plain crime anymore but massacre and baby snatching – *my* babies!'

Chris clanged the door shut and waited with folded arms.

The girl released one of the men suddenly, snatched at his gun. She missed it. He raised it, but not quickly enough for she raised the other man off his feet and flung him clean on top of the exploding weapon. He dropped, a hole burned through his chest.

Gun jolted from his hand the other man made a dash for it, until in two enormous leaps Vi caught up on him. He crashed to his knees, felt fingers of steel creep into his neck, tighter – tighter, until the cavern swam in a roaring tide . . .

Vi released him suddenly, stood up with a grim face. Turning she picked up the two rayguns, tossed one to Chris as he stood looking at her.

'Yes, they're dead,' she said curtly, interpreting his expression. 'Sorry to outrage those precious civilized notions of yours but I'm playing the game my way this time. I'll destroy this Welgand menace forever, or die doing it. Come on!'

She snatched open the metal door and together they hurried down the steps – but warily – to the next lens. Nobody intercepted them— So down to the main cavern floor where lay the tunnel-pit. A triggerman on guard suddenly jumped to his feet. That was as far as he got.

One hand knocked his gun flying; a fist shot out into his jaw and knocked him blinded and breathless against the cavern wall. Then Vi had him by the neck, forced him to stand upright.

'One chance for your life, ugly mug,' she breathed. 'Where's Welgand's power-room located? Come on, come on!' She slammed him mercilessly back and forth across the face as he hesitated.

'Wait – wait a minute! I'll show you— Lay off me! This way.'

'Hurry!' the girl snapped, her raygun ready.

The man fled before her and Chris across the cavern and to a low balcony of rock. A little way along it he stopped and pointed to a set of some twenty steps leading down to a metal door in a crevice below.

'In there?' Chris gasped. 'Hell! Rock and metal! It's invincible!'

'May not be; depends on this guy,' the girl retorted. She prodded him significantly. 'Go on, yell out. Tell Welgand he's wanted. Quick!'

The thug hesitated, measuring her, then he nodded and shouted loudly.

'Hey, Chief! Quick! Come on out—!'

The girl glanced towards the door to watch – and that was the movement the thug had been awaiting. Like a flash he landed out his fist, sent the girl spinning back against the rocky wall helplessly, her gun flying out of her hand. He started to run for it then, away along the gallery – but Chris was ready for that. He levelled his gun, fired. He felt a grim little thrill as he saw the smoky patch on the gangster's back. He dropped flat, motionless.

'Chris – out of sight!' Vi panted. 'Before Welgand

sees us. We've got to entice him out and slip in while he's away— Look out!'

They both flattened themselves in the shadow of the rocky wall as the power-room door in the crevice below opened. Welgand stood silhouetted against a glare from within. He waited. So did Vi and Chris, hoping against hope he'd come forward and investigate. Now they had lost their stooge they could do nothing to prompt him.

But at last, to their burning chagrin, he shrugged and went back in again, slammed the door resolutely.

CHAPTER III

DESPERATE STRAITS

'Damn!' Chris swore. 'Evidently he didn't think it was very important, else he didn't get all the words through that thick door. What do we do now? Reckoning three of these low-lifers out of the way there must be nine of 'em in with him. No others around here. How do we get him out?'

'I don't know.' Vi looked rather desperate. 'Time's flying too—'

Chris snapped his fingers. 'Welgand's spaceship! It's still in the cavern back there—'

'So what?'

'Get a raygun machine from it and melt that darned door down!'

'Um – he did blaze away with it back on Venus. Probably we could detach it—' Vi shook her dark head abruptly. 'No use. By the time we'd gotten through the door Welgand would be all set to blast us— But there's another angle to the ship,' she went on, turning and heading swiftly along the gallery. 'It has space radio. If we don't manage to break down that door, or anything should happen to us, we can at least warn Earth to stand clear of the eclipse track and evacuate those in its path.'

'Still doesn't solve how we bust that door open,' Chris said worriedly, hurrying beside her. 'We could imitate a voice to get him out only he might rumble the ruse—'

'We'll think of something: this is more important right now.'

In a few moments they were back in the main cavern, hurried over to where Welgand's ship still stood. It was all set and in order, space radio fully equipped. Chris closed the airlock for safety as the girl settled before the instruments and switched on.

'Welgand's radio will probably be in his power-house,' she reflected. 'Here's hoping he hasn't got it on so he won't know what we're up to here.'

She depressed the signal button on the Earth short-wave band and an answer soon came in the speaker. She cut it down to low tone.

'Calling Emergency Radio Station at Heaviside,' she intoned. 'This is the Golden Amazon speaking from the Moon. No time for explanations: just listen. Clear all people and valuables from the track of the total eclipse of the sun due to begin in about two hours. Dispatch an emergency squad at once to pick up Welgand, fugitive from Earth. That is all. Repeat please.'

The operator gave it back word for word. The girl broke contact, thought a moment, then said,

'May help to save plenty of lives anyway, if not all of them. Even at that millions of dollars' worth of property will go up in smoke unless we somehow get into that power room— We've got to do it suddenly, get Welgand off his guard so we can force the truth about the children out of him. Come on – see what we can do.'

'Bit queer he doesn't come to see what happened to those guys who came to look at the clock, isn't it?' Chris puzzled, as they returned along the narrow gallery.

Vi shrugged. 'Probably they're outside men – spend

their time in and around these galleries. He'll think they looked the job over and went back to their posts. Never suspect we got away.'

She paused as they came into the shadows of the gallery and stood looking down at the power-room door.

'Looks hopeless to me,' Chris muttered.

Vi did not reply immediately: she was studying the four massive pillars which supported the enormous quartz lens back in the cavern. Then as her gaze moved back to the gallery her eyes sharpened.

'Take a look . . .'

Chris stared at an immense boulder of rock jutting out of the rock face almost immediately behind them. It was enormous in size, like a pear-shaped protuberance.

'If that were free we might use it,' Vi murmured.

'What! Anyway, how do you propose to loosen it? It's too heavy to move even in this light gravity—'

'Might break it free with our rayguns.'

Vi set to work immediately and with a shrug Chris followed suit. They fired charge after charge at the pumice-like rock – silent shafts of flame that hurled dust and chippings into the air. Their guns were about burned out and useless when they had finished, but the rock around the boulder root had narrowed immensely.

The girl nodded when she had studied it, shoved at it. Nothing happened. She tried again, pushing mightily. There followed a cracking, splintering sound and the boulder, all of twenty feet high, dropped suddenly from its hold in the rock face and rolled ponderously for a short distance.

'Now what?' Chris demanded; then he looked worriedly at the rock face. 'Say, we've fissured it a hell of a lot. If the cracks widen at all—'

'Be hanged to that. Give me a hand.'

He only grasped what she was aiming at when their combined efforts edged the vast thing directly in line with the steps leading down to the power-room door. Then Vi pushed at it with her back, dug her heels in the floor and shoved. Once, twice— Three times. Then it toppled over the top step, sent her sprawling. Instantly she scrambled up and they both watched in awe as it pelted and bounced down the steps faster and faster—

It crashed into the metal door with cyclonic impact, ripped it clean off its hinges and took part of the frame with it.

'Now!' Vi yelled. 'Quick as you can go—'

She jumped as she spoke, went flying through the air and landed on the top of the now stationary boulder. In a moment she had slid down it and into the power-room. Without a second's hesitation she leapt again, clean on top of Welgand as he stood glancing round expectantly, obviously off his guard by the sudden onslaught.

He hardly had a chance, so fast did things happen. The girl's bunched fist struck him clean in the jaw as he waited with hand on his gun holster. Back of her blow was all the steel-spring strength of her supernatural muscles. Welgand lifted right off his feet, head jerked back and arms sprawling. He collided with a switchboard and brought up sharp. It saved him from falling. He let out a mighty yell.

Chris appeared suddenly, dived for the nearest gangster coming up to lend assistance. In a flying tackle Chris brought him to his knees. A lightning uppercut brought the man's teeth together with a click; he fell again, dazed and bewildered.

But now the place seemed to be spawning triggermen. The girl, clutching the dazed Welgand, found herself abruptly beleaguered with pointing rayguns. She whirled like lightning, gripped Welgand by his pants belt and held him in front of her as a shield.

'Okay,' she panted, raising him so that his feet kicked helplessly off the floor. 'It's up to you mugs now – Come over here, Chris! Up to you mugs, I say! First, where are those babies of mine—?' Then as the men scowled furiously she yelled, 'I'll give you five seconds! And I'm in no mood for niceties! Five seconds and I slam Welgand's head on the floor so hard it'll mash his brains—*Come on!*'

Welgand struggled desperately in her iron grip at the words. Her only response was to raise him even higher.

'One . . . !' she breathed implacably. 'Two—!'

'Hey, Amazon! Better take it easy!'

She looked up sharply beyond the nearer trigger-men to yet another gangster at the far end of the instrument-littered place. Her breath caught as she saw him holding the two babies on high, one in each hand.

'Checkmate!' he yelled. 'They're alive and kicking – but they won't be unless you release the Chief. Come on, get wise to yourself!'

Vi hesitated, in a quandary. Finally she released Welgand so abruptly he thumped to the floor. He got to his feet with a livid face, holding his anguishing jaw.

'If you know what's good for you you'll hand my babies over,' Vi snapped.

'What the hell do you think we are?' Welgand sneered. He glanced at the gangster. 'You hang onto 'em, Curly—'

'Why, you—'

Vi flung herself blindly towards the two children struggling in the man's hands, but this time sheer desperation upset her calculations. A foot shot out and tripped her. The next moment her arms were bent tightly behind her. Four of the gangsters pinned her down by main strength, panted and puffed as they bound her threshing limbs. At last she was pinioned, forced to her feet. She looked savagely across at Chris and beheld him in the same plight.

'I don't just know how you got away from that frame, Amazon,' Welgand said slowly, his voice deadly; 'but I do know you'll get no further than this power-room.

I'm taking no more chances. You can watch me operate the eclipse-ray from here. When that is done and you've seen the full layout of my vengeance I'll settle with you – fully!' He rubbed his jaw again furiously; it felt as though it were broken.

'Listen, Welgand,' Vi said, straining forward. 'I'm making no deals – that isn't my way; but I'll do anything you want if you'll only give my two kids a break. You said before that you'd killed them – I guessed that was for torture value, and now I've proved it. What do you want me to do?'

'There's nothing you can do to get out of this,' Welgand retorted. 'The only break either of you will get is in the neck— As for your two brats, I've got a future for them. I'll bring them up my way—'

'*Your* way!' Vi shouted. 'Crime, villainy, murder—'

'*My* way,' Welgand repeated stonily. 'They're exceptional kids, being yours. A boy and a girl of a superrace to come – the strength of ten men. Venus-reared – swift, intelligent, cruel and terrible as the sabre toothed tiger if trained the right way – *my* way. Your kids, Amazon! What better vengeance than that their whole lives be devoted to the very thing you have tried to destroy? I foresee a superrace of men and women under my orders. Good eh?' Welgand grinned tauntingly, then he remembered his jaw and winced instead.

'You'll not make it, Welgand,' the girl whispered. 'I'll get you somehow. Even if you kill me I'll come back. I'll break you in the end! Those are my babies – a new race, yes – but destined to found an empire of magnificent man and womanhood between them when I get too old to fight anymore. You shall not have them!'

'That's what you think,' Welgand answered callously; then he glanced at his watch. 'Anyway, I've no time for argument. Eclipse time is in ten minutes. Make yourselves comfortable,' he added dryly, as they stood pinioned helplessly before him.

Bitterly they stood watching as he turned to his control

board. It was not particularly elaborate, was obviously meant to operate an immense level-mechanism at the far end of the laboratory.

'This moves the shields aside from the lenses,' Welgand said in explanation. 'It— You listening, Amazon?'

She jerked her eyes from the two infants still in the grip of the grinning trigger-man farther down the laboratory.

'I heard you, yes,' she retorted. 'You pull the shields aside, the sun sends its power through the tunnel and—'

'In exactly eight more minutes,' Welgand nodded. 'Then . . .'

He paused, frowning a little as from somewhere there came a dull cracking sound. It was followed by a heavy rumbling bump – then silence.

'What was that?' He wheeled round on his men.

'Only some rocks tumbling away when you moved the shield, I guess,' one of them answered.

Welgand reflected, then nodded. He closed another switch and a window on the far wall sprang into view as a steel shutter shot back. Beyond it was dead black.

'There you see the inside of the shaft,' he explained. 'You will see the sunlight pass up it— Ah! Notice that pearly haze? That is the beginning!'

Breathing hard, Chris and Vi waited. The girl strained and tugged at her cords as she watched first the snicking clock over the switchboard and then the gathering glow on the inspection-window. She knew there could never have been time on Earth to clear everybody out of the way to safety. Havoc beyond imagination would be inevitable the instant the umbra of the eclipse struck the Earth.

She pulled again, tautened her arms – then her eyes caught sight of Curly holding the babies. He shook his head negatively. It was a threat – possibly bluff – but Vi realized she could take no chances. Again she relaxed, wishing she could not hear the merciless click – click – click of the timepiece.

Welgand and his men stood in ghoulish satisfaction as the pearly glow deepened. It became creamy, then white; until at last the first direct ray streamed through. Instantly the window became blindingly brilliant as the effulgence poured up the shaft.

'Wonderful!' Welgand breathed. 'My supreme moment! The consummation of four years' hard work.'

'Yeah, you said it, Chief!'

'Serve those boiled shirt scientists right!'

'If ever there was a dirty rotten swine, it's you, Welgand,' Chris panted. 'You ought to be damned well—'

Welgand reached forward, slapped Chris across the face with such force that he fell helplessly on his back. He turned and glared up – then Welgand's eyes shifted to the girl. He met the steely stare of her deep blue eyes.

'Better lay off me, Welgand,' she breathed. 'You've already done enough. If I ever catch up on you—!'

'Not where you're going, Amazon,' Welgand said calmly. 'I've one more surprise to spring on you – and this weak-kneed husband of yours. That window opens inward into the shaft—'

Vi looked at it, startled.

'You guessed it,' Welgand commented grimly. 'I decided you should die by the same system that destroyed my Earthly foes. That you escaped the lenses does not mean you will escape the method— The concentrated heat down that moon shaft will kill you, slowly – far more slowly than would have been the case on the lens. Both of you will die in that shaft. I guess you crossed me for the last time, Amazon!'

He waited a moment, added shortly, 'Okay, boys – go to it.'

Two of the men moved instantly, hauled the girl up between them and carried her struggling, wriggling form to the window, dropped her under it by the wall. Then they did the same for Chris. Welgand came up, yanked the girl up by her ropes and grinned at her taut, furious face.

'Bit of a come-down for the mighty Amazon, eh?' he asked dryly; then his face setting like granite he raised her suddenly in his arms to the level of the window. Her feet indeed were pressing on the glass when something happened— It was so sudden it drowned out Chris' wild cry of alarm.

It sounded like a vast explosion from somewhere above the power-room and was followed by a crumbling, grumbling roar that rose with the seconds and set the floor shaking. Small rocks began to bounce through the shattered doorway and rolled across the floor; clouds of choking dust followed them.

'A moonquake!' Curly yelled hoarsely, springing up. 'Quick, Chief, we've gotta get outa here—'

Welgand looked round in alarm, then dropped the helpless girl back to the floor. In his anxiety he seemed suddenly oblivious to his heinous scheme of destruction and vengeance. Thinking only of himself now he raced across the quivering floor as the din increased, snatched the two children from the arms of the running Curly, and with one bound was with them over the rock blocking the door.

He was the only one that got through. The hell exploded suddenly into an onslaught of stones and rock, burying not only Curly but the rest of the men as they made belated moves to reach safety.

CHAPTER IV

SETTLING OF ACCOUNTS

'Looks bad, Vi,' Chris panted, squirming to free himself. 'We—'

'Lie flat!' the girl shouted hoarsely, glancing up suddenly, and simultaneously she pressed herself as low as possible to the floor.

Not a second too soon for the immense laboratory roof suddenly split its entire length, demolished itself in a hail of rocks and boulders that crumbled inward. The whole Moon seemed to be sliding and shifting. Chris winced as the pumicey stuff rained down on top of him, burying him, filling his mouth and ears with dust and chippings. Bound as he was he found himself utterly pinned when at last the disturbance began to show signs of ending.

'Vi!' His voice was choked and muffled. 'Vi, you still around?'

'Yeah – lie still a moment . . .'

Then Chris heard the crack and clink of stone as the girl heaved and twisted herself out of the mass. In a while he heard her laboured breathing . . . then the pressure upon him began to lighten as she flung away the stones at top speed, finally dragged him to his feet. He saw broken ends of cord clinging now along with the manacle cuffs to her wrists and ankles.

'Won't be a second,' she panted, and snapped his cords through like string. 'Easy enough to escape these cords now the rayguns are not trained on us— Guess we can thank the light gravity for not being crushed under this lot— There! We're ready!'

Chris stared round him dazedly. The laboratory was a shambles. The entire roof had fallen in, leaving it open to the cavern beyond. Here and there an arm or leg sticking from the debris testified to the fate of the rest of Welgand's stooges.

'Don't know whether they're dead or not – no time to look,' Vi snapped. 'Welgand got the kids and that's all we need to know—'

She caught Chris' arm and they blundered across the fallen rubble into the cavern. Now they saw more clearly what had happened. One of the four immense rock pillars supporting the lowest quartz lens had snapped in two, bringing down half the wall with it.

'A miniature cataclysm,' Chris breathed. 'Say, that rock we pulled out must have started it. I warned you about that fissure—'

Vi did not even seem to notice. She stared at the blank space where Welgand's ship had been.

'Gone! I expected it— He wouldn't stop to move the *Ultra* anyway, so that's our last hope. Come on!'

'We've no spacesuits, though,' Chris exclaimed, as he followed her up the shaft giving egress to the surface.

'We're going to chance it,' she retorted. 'You can stay here if you want. I'm stronger than you.'

Had he not known her brutal frankness was born of desperation he'd have answered hotly. As it was he remained silent, but followed just the same.

'It won't be easy,' Vi said, as they went on up. 'It means a brief climb and a run in sheer void and zero cold – but it can be done! Free space is a perfect insulator of heat; you radiate heat faster than it can escape. A body can stay in space for a while without bursting: depends how strong the body is— Yes, I can risk it. The slighter gravity will help in making a prodigious dash.'

She stopped speaking as the trap was reached. She tugged it down, hesitated a second, then plunged through. Chris followed her – into hell. Blinding cold wrapped him immediately. He felt the searing vacuum of the airless lunar night, gulped and struggled to hold his breath. He floundered, almost fell, his head singing with iron bands clamped round it.

He was dimly aware that the girl stooped, whipped him up and bundled him up the remainder of the rocky slope: then holding onto him tightly she leapt – once, twice – three times, hurled by her more than human leg muscles. But even she was weakening noticeably as she fumbled through the *Ultra*'s outer airlock.

Chris floundered through the last airlock and lay gulping on the control room floor. He looked up blearily as the girl followed him, spun the lock screws. Blood was trickling from her nose.

'Guess it's the last time I want to try that,' she panted. 'I thought I was going to blow apart any minute— Get the restorative out while I pick up that scum, Welgand.'

By the time Chris had handed over the glass of restorative the girl had the *Ultra* sweeping over the Tycho crater. She glanced below momentarily.

'Looks as though that quake put Welgand's infernal mirror out of focus anyway,' she said briefly. 'No sign of a ray, even though there is an eclipse cone— Ah! There he is!' Her eyes narrowed vengefully as she stared ahead.

'Heading to Venus,' Chris murmured. 'I get it! He thinks we passed out and figures on taking the kids there to bring them up where they can get the Venusian radiation—' He paused as he looked rearwards. 'Hallo! Space patrol – Earth ships. Heading Moonward—'

'The ones I sent for,' Vi nodded. She switched on her space radio. 'Hallo there, Earth patrol! Amazon calling – *Ultra* about a hundred miles ahead of you. Drop two parties to look over the lunar interior setup; the rest of you follow me as well as you can. Welgand has got away again.'

'Say, Amazon, what goes on?' demanded an officer's voice. 'We cleared all the folks out of the eclipse track – many as we could anyway. We were in space when the eclipse began. That ray showed momentarily then veered off sideways and went out—'

'No time to explain now,' Vi retorted. 'Follow me!'

She switched off, clamped her hand down on the power lever and set it moving up notch by notch. With terrific overpowering speed the little machine whizzed ever faster through the void, eating up the distance, leaving the police squad far behind as their numbers broke up.

'More distance we can cover before Welgand gets wise that we're on his tail the better,' Vi panted.

'More ahead we are of the police the better, too. This is my tea-party, and no hounds of the law are going to spoil it. Just wait!'

She slipped the lever to the last notch, hardly seemed to notice the appalling pressure so tense was her whole being on the job of settling accounts with the fleeing scientist.

Welgand's space machine, fast though it was, began to lose ground to the *Ultra*. At first it was a puzzle to Vi, then she snapped her fingers. 'Because of the children!' she exclaimed. 'He dare not use full power. Last time he had a vast head start which kept him ahead; this time he hasn't . . . Hallo, what's that?'

Evidently he had become aware of pursuit for from the rear of his machine there suddenly blazed the livid flare of a raygun.

'I guessed he'd do that,' the girl muttered, plunging dizzily to miss the long-distance beam. 'He knows I can't hit back in case we blow the kids up too.'

She swerved again, careened in a mighty arc. Her jaw set as she heard one of the *Ultra*'s outer plates go tearing off under a transient glancing blast of withering fire. And now she was commencing to overtake Welgand's machine in leaps and bounds: she cut speed a little, manipulated the rocket controls with all the skill at her command to dodge his repeated fire.

'Just what do you figure on doing, Vi?' Chris demanded, rising up from the wall bed as the speed decreased. 'We can't keep up this cat and dog act forever: he'll blast our vitals for sure with a lucky hit. Then what?'

'I've got the thing figured,' she answered quickly. 'I can't blast his ship itself, but I *can* blast his airlock. There are three of 'em, remember. Once I've opened the outer one I'll get through the other two in double quick time—'

'But he'll guess the idea!'

'No; that's where you come in.' She sprang up and

motioned to the control board. Chris took over the controls as she scrambled into a space suit.

'Your job is to distract his attention,' she went on earnestly. 'Keep his aim fixed on this ship: do all you can to dodge him. Leave the rest to me. This is my personal job!'

Before Chris could say anything she screwed on her helmet, picked up a heavy sub-standard raygun and fastened it to her waist. Carefully she made her way to the emergency lock away from the view of Welgand's machine; then slipped herself out into space and hung onto her lifeline.

Automatically the gravity of the *Ultra* kept her close to it. She waited, hanging onto the rope while Chris writhed and plunged the ship around, manoeuvring at last so that he came up under the belly of Welgand's machine.

Vi was waiting for that vital second. She thrust her feet against the *Ultra* and the recoil whizzed her across the briefly narrow gap. Simultaneously she let go of her lifeline and clung onto the projections round Welgand's ship's airlock. She was pretty sure he had not seen her, busy as he was at the rear of the vessel and with its external centre hidden from his view.

Smiling grimly inside her helmet Vi hooked one arm around the lock hinge and went to work with the heavy gun. White heat blistered round the clamps of the operculum. Metal began to flow in a white hot pool as the machine continued to hurtle onwards through the void. Time and again the *Ultra* came whizzing round, plunging and sweeping the abyss. Far away the police squad was commencing to catch up—

Then the lock gave. The girl slid inside the vessel quickly, whipped out her ordinary raygun and held it tightly. As she had hoped, the second airlock was double levered, openable from inside and out. She went past it quickly, shut it and took off her helmet. The last door faced her.

Abruptly she flung it open—

'Reach, Welgand!'

Welgand, the two infants on chairs on either side of him, swung around violently from his raygun mechanism. An astounded expression came over his cruel vindictive visage.

'Amazon! How in hell did you—?'

He raised his arms slowly and the girl moved forward; then even as she did so his left hand dropped and whipped out his gun. He upped and fired simultaneously from the hip.

His guess was right in one sense: the girl did not dare fire back in case she hit her babies: but Welgand's own lightning movement was too swift. He blistered paint and metal on the wall beside the girl as she leapt like a tigress to one side—

Nor did she stop leaping. She jumped again the moment she hit the floor, tossed her gun on the switchboard bench and lammed out with her right fist.

It caught Welgand on his already injured jaw just a fraction of a second after he had tried to dodge. The result was he spun like a top, his gun flying out of his fist. He reached for his remaining right-hand gun but it was too late. Vi's hand closed round his wrist like a vice, exerted a crushing pressure that grew worse with the seconds. His face lifted in anguish and round came her fist clean into it, sent him hurtling backwards helplessly against the wall.

He brought up with a jolt that shook his teeth. His hair was tumbled; he was sweating violently. He realized now he was not looking on a woman at all, but the real superhuman jungle female who at heart was still a savage of the Venusian jungles. Her face was the nearest thing to a human tigress he had ever seen.

'We've a score to settle, Welgand – a long outstanding one,' she said in a low voice. 'You were going to steal my babies, poison their lives, make super-criminals out of them. I warned you what would happen when I caught up with you—'

'Wait, Amazon – wait a minute!' Welgand fought for breath. 'We can settle this thing without violence. You don't have to be a murderess—'

Vi wasted no more time on his panicky drooling. Frantically though he tried to avoid her she vaulted after him, right and left across the control room, caught up on him and brought him to his knees at last with her forearm hooked under his chin. Her knee crushed mercilessly into the small of his back. He recognized that favourite hold of hers – a strangling backward pressure that no human being had ever yet escaped.

'Amazon! *Amazon!*' he screamed huskily, choking. 'In God's name—!'

Tighter her arm closed, and tighter. Welgand could no longer speak. The world was roaring in his anguished ears – flaming pain burned the length of his spine— Then amazingly the whole thing relaxed and he tumbled spent and gasping to the floor.

He had an idea there were voices, furious cries from the girl. He shook his befuddled head and got up slowly, quivering still from the expectancy of death that had gripped him. Now he saw the sullen, bitter faced girl in the grip of a party of police officers – space police. And Chris Wilson himself.

'What's the idea?' Vi blazed, glaring around. 'Want this guy to escape as he did last time? Let me finish the job! He's got to die!'

'Not at your hands, though, Vi,' Chris insisted. 'That's plain jungle law – and there are proper laws. You've got to obey them.'

Welgand stood listening, rubbing his aching neck. He dropped his hand to the switchboard bench to support himself – and his hand dropped right on the girl's gun. Surprised he looked at it; then he whipped it up – but Vi was a second quicker seeing his action a shade sooner.

She ripped free of the now lax grip on her arms, bunched her right fist and drove it out like a piston rod.

Even one of her feet left the floor with the terrific power she put behind it. It was the most astounding punch Chris had ever seen, and he'd seen plenty. Just as though she had blown everything in one vast colossal effort.

Welgand's head jerked back like a punch-bag. His teeth clicked loudly. He shot rather than toppled away from the group, crashed into the opposite wall with his mouth welling blood. Like a rag doll he crumpled motionless to the floor.

'Whew, was that dynamite!' Chris whistled, as the girl stood shaking her hand painfully.

'Should have been,' she replied fervently. 'I've broken three of my knuckles.'

The officer-in-charge went over to Welgand and studied him briefly. He got up and shrugged.

'Broken neck,' he said briefly. 'Either the punch or else the switchboard.'

'But it was self-defence,' the girl said slowly. 'It was not murder. He pulled a gun on us. Right?'

The officer nodded slowly, gave a grim smile. 'Saved the Earth a job of work, Amazon. But you'd better watch yourself in future with those muscles of yours. May get you into trouble.'

'Not again,' she answered quietly. 'That was probably my last big wallop. I'm all through fighting now Welgand's washed-up. My next fights will be domestic – training these two kids of mine to become the forerunners of a super race.'

The officer smiled again as she picked the children up in her strong arms, petted them affectionately.

'Anyway,' he said, thinking, 'that'll be twenty years from now and I won't be on the space force then. If they're anything like their mother I'll count that in my favour. But joking aside, Amazon, you've finished a masterly job. Good luck to you – in fact all four of you!'

Origin of a Superhero

by Donald F. Glut

The silvery wheelchair jetted across the ancient wooden drawbridge, shaking the skinny frame of the old man manipulating its controls. Bertram Starr had paid a small fortune for the swiftly moving conveyance, but to a man of his wealth such extravagance barely made an impression on his reserve capital. Besides, the wheelchair was not a luxury but a necessity. His bony legs had been crippled since birth and such a device had proved to be still the most efficient means of locomotion for the handicapped, even in the early years of the twenty-first century.

Starr looked up into the sky as he was ferried along. There were no clouds that afternoon and the warm sunlight beamed down upon him from an overhead sea of azure. He watched the looming time- and weather-eroded towers of the anachronistic medieval castle eclipse the sun as he glided smoothly forward. It was a fine day for the experiment, he reassured himself once more.

Odd, he thought, as he brought the wheelchair to a noiseless halt in front of the relatively new steel door, that such fortresses should still exist after so many centuries. Yet this structure, rising like some monolithic stone god from the hilltop just outside the town of Ingoldstadt, in what had once been known as Bavaria, had successfully resisted the passage of years, just as it had once resisted the assault of besieging armies.

He raised a frail hand to the photoelectric cell mounted on the doorframe and interrupted the invisible beam of light. A humming sound, then the door slid silently open, retreating into a slot cut into the wall itself. A touch of a button on the wheelchair's control panel and he was propelled forward into the castle.

When the wheelchair next rolled to a halt, Starr was in the elaborate laboratory his fortune had paid for five years previously. Much had happened during those years, he reflected. His millions had financed the establishment of new schools and universities, the construction of new hospitals, had even brought medical science to the brink of discovering a cure for cancer, and contributed to the salvation and restoration of many of Earth's natural resources. Starr liked to think that the clear blue sky outside the castle owed its existence, at least in part, to his riches.

He gazed about the laboratory. Even with the sunlight blazing in through one window, and the harsh artificial lighting, there was still a tangible gloominess about the place. No doubt some of this depressing atmosphere was due to the stone-walls, dark and chipped, that not even the laboratory apparatus – apparatus that appeared futuristic even by twenty-first century standards – could not entirely camouflage. Yet, even more than its daunting physical appearance, what really gave the place its sinister ambience were the tragic memories associated with it.

No one had been more affected by those memories than the middle-aged man in the white laboratory smock now approaching the man in the wheelchair from a shadowy alcove.

'Right on time, Mister Starr,' he welcomed.

'I'm always on time, Viktor,' said Starr with an impatient but not unamused smile. 'You didn't really expect me to be late *today* did you? On this so *very* special occasion?' He felt a wave of delight at the realization that his money would finally bring the great experiment to its conclusion that very afternoon.

Starr's sunken chest swelled for a few moments as it almost invariably did when he accomplished some new benevolence for his fellow man. He was old now, pushing ninety-three, and not in the best of health by anyone's standards. But he had lived as beneficially as he could a life that another might have wasted; especially given so vast a fortune.

'You know,' said Bertram Starr, cruising the laboratory, admiring the scientific wonders his wealth had purchased, 'I've always loved people . . . I've always wanted to do whatever was in my power to help my fellow human beings. When I was younger I dreamed of becoming a doctor or a teacher or a missionary, taking health and knowledge to people in countries less fortunate than my own . . . But nature – or Fate or God, if you will – has seen to it that I can only help my fellow man indirectly – from afar.'

Viktor caught himself staring at the frozen legs of the man in the wheelchair, and looked quickly away. 'But you've spent every penny you possibly could to benefit mankind,' he said to cover his embarrassment.

Starr nodded thoughtfully. 'I've tried, Viktor, Heaven knows I've tried . . .' He spun the wheelchair round so he could look directly up into the scientist's lined face. Though he knew it would be useless, he again made a determined effort to move his legs. After several seconds of straining, he slumped, struggling to catch his breath. There was no reason for legs that had not moved since birth to begin now.

'But somehow,' Starr resumed, his face showing emotion not entirely due to his exertion, 'it wasn't quite the same. I mean, no matter how many dollars I poured into the countless charities and worthy causes that came my way – and they *were* countless, Viktor – it was not the same as my getting up out of this confounded rolling prison and doing some good myself, with these own two hands of mine . . . But that's been an idle wish, Viktor. There's not a doctor on this Earth been able to get me walking on my own two feet, let alone developing this feeble carcass of mine to the point where I could do anything you could call . . . well, let's say, *heroic*.'

'And that's where I come in, Mister Starr,' said Viktor softly. 'And your wealth, of course,' he added with appropriate gratitude.

Starr saw the irony, and allowed himself a tight-lipped smile. 'That's right, Viktor,' he said. 'What might very well turn out to be the last "donation" of a dying man could actually be the one act that gets me free of this damn chair – and doing the things I've dreamed about doing ever since I was a boy. Ever since . . .' For a brief moment he fell into silent recollection, his eyes gleaming. 'I don't suppose you've ever heard of them, Viktor,' he said finally, 'but we had something back then we called comic books . . .'

'I've seen some of them,' said Viktor. 'On display in America in the Marshall Natural History Museum's rare book department. But I never actually read any of them. They're all collector's items now. Even the ones from the 1990s are much too rare and valuable for the likes of me.'

'Well, I read as many as I can get my crippled hands on,' said the millionaire. 'Even ones from the so-called "Golden Age" of the 1940s. Of course, they've had to be chemically treated – those which hadn't already disintegrated before the end of the century. And I read many comic books when they were new. There were all kinds . . . but those that had the most appeal – especially to someone like me, who couldn't even *walk* – were those about the superheroes. Ah, how I fancied myself in the role of Superman, the Mighty Man of Steel, soaring through the skies with red cape streaming, using my superhuman powers to fight evil and avert disaster!'

'Yes,' said Viktor, 'I guess everyone's heard of Superman. Even today he's still a household word. I suppose he must have been the original?'

'And sometimes, in my fantasies,' Starr continued, as if he had momentarily forgotten Viktor's presence, 'I became Captain Marvel, who was as powerful as Superman but who was really young Billy Batson until he shouted the word *Shazam!* And Captain America –

a weakling chemically transformed into a super-soldier dressed in red, white and blue . . . And I'll never forget the thrill I experienced each time Dr Donald Blake stomped his walking stick and became golden-haired Thor, the Norse God of Thunder. Or the vicarious excitement I felt when young Chuck Chandler put on the special glasses that let him become the 3-D Man in the powerful body of his older brother. And speaking of brothers, I'll never forget my favourite of them all – the Fighting American, who was another composite character, a rebuilt dead man brought back to life with the transplanted mind of his younger brother . . . How I dreamed of being able to help mankind the way my heroes did, my crippled body miraculously transformed and energized with superhuman powers! And now, thanks to your genius . . .'

'And your money, Mr Starr . . .'

'*And* my money,' Starr agreed, 'that may soon be possible.' He looked suddenly around the laboratory, searching. 'But where is—?'

Viktor moved quickly across the room and drew back an opaque plastic curtain directly behind the millionaire. Starr depressed the button which powered his wheelchair to make a 180 degree turn. His eyes widened at what he saw as he gazed upwards.

It stood silent, unmoving, an awesome humanoid form encased in a glassoid dome. The creature was a veritable giant, at least eight feet tall, and its body, sleek and silvery, was that of a broad-shouldered Hercules. The face had been handsomely sculpted and, but for its silver hue, might have passed for human. The scarlet boots, trunks and wristbands gave the impression of a uniform or costume, as did the silver insignia emblazoned on a large red diamond in the centre of the creature's powerful chest.

'Alpha-One,' said Starr, contemplating the insignia, a Greek letter and a Roman numeral. He said the two words slowly, reverently, as though standing in the presence of some frozen god awaiting the spark of life. Which in a way he was.

'To think what we might have accomplished, Viktor, had there been an Alpha-One in earlier decades,' Starr enthused.

The smile on Viktor's face faded as he approached the silent silver being, dwarfed by its height and powerful frame. Sombrely he said, 'To think it would take all these years, all these *centuries*, not just to save mankind, but to restore the honour of my family name.'

'Many of my ancestors were forced to change their name for their own safety,' he continued, staring into the immobile features of the silver giant, 'but I kept mine because I had faith that this day would come.' He turned away so Starr could not see the intensity of his emotion.

Starr eased the wheelchair forward until he was at Viktor's side. 'I understand, Viktor,' he said. 'I imagine that going through life with the name of Frankenstein must have been almost as unbearable as having to live in this crippled body of mine. Well, perhaps today will see both our problems solved. Permanently.'

Viktor gestured towards the laboratory's ancient stone walls. 'It was in this very castle, in the late eighteenth century, that my ancestor, Victor Frankenstein, created the so-called Monster. Since that day, the name of Frankenstein has been scorned, ridiculed and linked to the most unspeakable horrors – and, who knows, perhaps rightly so. But today, I'm going to exonerate the family name once and for all!'

'Your ancestor created his monster by grafting together pieces from individual corpses and gave it life with chemicals and electricity—'

'And inadvertently created a living monstrosity that soon destroyed all he loved!' Viktor cut in. 'But this time,' he went on, returning his gaze to the face of the silver giant, 'it will be different because I've avoided my ancestor's mistakes. This time the body is not made from dead bodies and animal tissue but from an indestructible shell of plastic fluid. This time he is not some junkyard zombie but an android, perfect in every way, and with powers to rival those of any of your cherished comic book characters. And this time his mind will not be that of an executed murderer but of our century's greatest humanitarian!'

Starr dipped his head modestly. 'Thank you, Viktor . . . Yet whatever I may have accomplished in the past won't even begin to compare with the good that will result from your achievement today.'

'If we are successful,' said Viktor.

The android called Alpha-One loomed high above Starr. It seemed to be waiting for him to surrender that part of himself which would result in the creation of the all-powerful being that was to be the new Saviour of mankind. In a way, the glass-encased humanoid reminded Starr of one of his favourite superheroes, the original Human Torch, an android which had promptly burst into flame upon receiving his first taste of artificial life. And, of course, he thought of the Fighting American, brought to life in a similar experiment to the one that was about to take place inside Castle Frankenstein.

'Well,' said Starr, 'the sun is out there waiting for us. It isn't going to get any brighter . . . So if you're ready, I most certainly am.'

Viktor waved his hand before another of the castle's many photoelectric eyes. A section of the ceiling at once opened to admit the noon brightness into the laboratory. Giant mirrors, paid for by Starr's fortune, slowly turned to best receive the sudden influx of sunlight. In its glow, the android's metallic body shone even more brightly.

Starr was fully aware what he had to do next; he and Viktor had rehearsed it often enough. For several seconds he gazed contemptuously down on his body, old and weak and crippled. Good riddance, he thought, then rapidly wheeled himself beneath another, smaller glassoid dome. He saw Viktor's hand move out to interrupt another light-beam, this one causing the dome to descend until it completely covered the wheelchair and its occupant. Less than a minute later, Viktor Frankenstein was pulling a massive lever, precipitating the last and most crucial phase of his experiment.

For a full sixty seconds, Bertram Starr was trapped within the core of the Sun itself. Or so it seemed to the man in the wheelchair. Frankenstein, his laboratory, the castle, even the dome – all were washed away in an ocean of blinding radiance. Briefly Starr felt acute pain jolting through his body like thousands of volts of electricity. And then all unpleasant sensations were gone as the consciousness of the aged millionaire was suddenly plunged into – *nothing*. Complete infinite emptiness. Even the Sun's brilliance had blanked out. Then his awareness seemed to rise endlessly through dimension after dimension of unreality, at last coming to rest . . . he wasn't sure *where*.

Reality slowly returned.

All was peaceful now, peaceful and silent. Bertram Starr rediscovered himself. Instinctively he felt he had the ability to move, even to walk, but he remained motionless, afraid even when he heard the low humming which he knew to be the raising of the domes, and the section of ceiling returning to its former position.

Starr's hearing was keen now, keener than it had ever been in his entire life, and he distinctly heard Viktor's normally quiet footsteps as the scientist approached. When he willed it, Starr found he could hear Viktor's heartbeat, the bellows-like sound of his lungs, even the flutter of his eyelids.

'I think we've done it, Mr Starr!' boomed Viktor's excited voice. 'I think the experiment was a success! Can you move? Can you open your eyes?'

Bertram Starr toned down the extreme sensitivity of his hearing until Viktor's words reached him at a tolerable level. He mused to himself that he could switch off the sound altogether if he chose. He did not immediately respond to Frankenstein's entreaties. He was revelling in the unaccustomed sensation of *height*, the incredible feeling that he was no longer seated in his accursed wheelchair. And he no longer felt the urge, even the need, to breathe . . .

Starr opened his eyes.

Beneath him, he saw Viktor Frankenstein smiling, obviously beside himself with satisfaction at his achievement. Beneath him! No one had ever stood *beneath* him before . . . But it was not Viktor he was anxious to see. With liquid ease he turned his head to view a familiar yet lifeless husk, slumped over in a jet-powered wheelchair. Then the being that now housed Bertram Starr's consciousness smiled.

'No longer are you Bertram Starr!' shouted Frankenstein, with a touch, at least, of the madness that had afflicted certain of his ancestors through the centuries. 'From this moment, you are the first of a new breed of Super-man! You are . . . *Alpha-One!*'

Alpha-One lowered his head to look upon his silver hands, either one of which had the capability of averting a million disasters or smashing whatever spectres of evil plagued the Earth. Looking straight ahead, he took his first steps – the first steps Bertram Starr had ever known. As he moved he could feel his artificially created body pulsing with the amplified power of the Sun. When he reached the laboratory's full-length mirror, he saw an eight-foot silver and crimson superhero staring majestically back at him.

For a moment he reflected on the good that Alpha-One could accomplish, even today, the very first day of his existence in the world of *homo-sapiens*.

Alpha-One turned to his creator. He spoke and, even though he was equipped to speak with any voice he chose, his voice was that of Bertram Starr.

'I feel . . .' he began, then paused as he clenched his fists and felt them crackle with the energies of a hundred suns. 'I feel like I could do anything . . . *Anything!*'

'And so you can,' said Viktor Frankenstein with

pride. 'You have inestimable strength, limitless power, and I've constructed your body to be immortal as well as totally indestructible. Not only have I created the one being who can save this world from the follies of the human race, but I've also absolved the good name of Frankenstein!'

Alpha-One was most anxious to begin his mission, for the desire to help mankind was already welling up within his artificial heart. The massive steel door tore easily from its frame in the superhero's hand; no matter, he would repair it later. All that mattered now was that he had to test the powers Frankenstein had given him. Seconds later he was soaring into the clear blue sky with the speed of a rocket, leaving his creator and Castle Frankenstein far below.

Like a silver dart, he tore through the clouds bunched above the Bavarian Alps. With the heat that blasted through his fingertips, he melted a tunnel before him as he shot through the peaks of the highest mountains. With his fists he punched his way through the Earth itself. And with his supersensitive faculties, he was a party to the most private actions and secret whispers of anyone he chose to observe.

Alpha-One was power incarnate and he knew it.

Even as he accomplished his marvels, Alpha-One's human personality was at work, his thoughts filtering through a perfect android brain. He remembered that for every humane act his money had bought, there had always been someone in the background sneering at his helplessness. With sudden vivid insight he recalled his very first act of philanthropy as it really was, not prompted by an insatiable desire to help mankind, but by a desire to end the ridicule of a crippled boy and buy himself some popularity. Alpha-One realized what Bertram Starr had managed to forget – that the charity of man's greatest benefactor was actually the most efficient means at his disposal of making himself acceptable to his fellow man.

Fellow man?

Alpha-One gazed downward, contemplating the miniscule patches of colour that made up the patterns of the Earth. He soared higher, until the blueness of the heavens were drowned in the blackness of space. The universe was Alpha-One's and the stars were within his silver grasp.

Fellow man! The notion brought a curl of contempt to Alpha-One's lips – for now he had no fellow men. He was unique in the universe, a superhuman being who could challenge the gods. No, he was himself a god, one with the power to reshape the Earth according to his whim, to either dominate or destroy its inferior ruling race.

As a streak of silver shot back down towards the Earth, the human consciousness of Bertram Starr knew happiness.

He would first return to Castle Frankenstein, where the only mortal who had knowledge of his true origin would be the first to know his fury! He lashed through the sky until the medieval castle appeared beneath him. Alpha-One laughed as he plunged towards it. For, as Viktor had so cleverly predicted, this time things would indeed be different . . .

Worse, in fact, by a billionfold.

Captain Amazing

by Stephen Hitchcock

Captain Amazing could easily have overtaken the hijacked security van with two of his stupendous leaps, but he never liked getting too close where gold was concerned, and he knew the security van was carrying $600,000 in gold bars. Instead of pursuing he tore down a lamp standard and hurled it like a javelin after the speeding van. As always, his aim was true and the lamp standard, hitting the van's rear axle with tremendous force, shattered the transmission shaft into cast-iron confetti and wrenched the axle itself into a perfect U-shape, making both back wheels spin off in opposite directions. One of the wheels headed for a small girl who happened to be standing at the kerb sucking a frosticle, her eyes wide. Captain Amazing snatched her out of the way just in time and set her down in safety. 'Wow, *thank you*, Captain Amazing,' she breathed, offering him a bite of her frosticle.

But the Captain had no time to dally. While on his way to intercept the stolen security van, his ever-alert supersensitive hearing had detected suspicious sounds coming from the main vault of a neighbourhood bank. With a single effortless bound, he leapt into the sky, heading back to investigate . . .

'This renegade must obviously be stopped,' said the Chairman of the High Council of Sirius-D. 'Instead of promoting the Sirian ideal of the superior individual, he is using his Sirian powers to thwart all ingenuity and initiative on Earth. It is only these "villains" he fights who show any sign of the originality and independence of mind which Earthling civilization needs if it is to survive. But we must not only stop this so-called Captain Amazing, we must also discredit him, so as to undo some of the damage he has done.

'This is what I propose we should do. As you know, the Earthlings are obsessed by this substance "gold". We shall use their obsession against the renegade. We shall go down to Earth with all the force we can muster. A small party which I myself shall lead will arrest Captain Amazing and bring him back to Sirius-D to stand trial. The rest of the expeditionary force, dressed in copies of the traitor's distinctive uniform, and acting as individual units, will raid every national bank and gold reserve on Earth and will transport this *gold* substance to a number of large cargo-ships waiting in the middle of the great open space the Earthlings call the Sahara Desert. We will plant evidence in one of these spaceships incriminating Captain Amazing and leave it behind when we fly home. When these pitiful Earthlings eventually take stock of what has happened they will jump to the obvious conclusion – that their precious Captain Amazing has made off with their gold!'

He sat back, smiling modestly as the members of the High Council rose to their feet and applauded.

After winding up the Baker Bay Bullion Smuggling Case by delivering the Minelli Gang to the 11th Precinct copshop, Captain Amazing headed home to his secret apartment in a Bronx tenement, knowing that tomorrow would bring yet another signed testimonial from the President to put with the others in the bottom drawer of his wardrobe. In his apartment he changed out of his platinum leotards into slacks, sweatshirt and sneakers. If it hadn't been for the insane desire of so many Earthlings to accumulate such large quantities of gold for their own private use, instead of leaving it in Fort Knox where it did least harm, Captain Amazing would have always worn slacks, sweatshirt and sneakers. Captain Amazing loved Earth and had no more sincere wish than to live with the Earthlings as an equal, accepted by them as one of themselves. If only the criminal elements would let him do that. He didn't object to all villains as such; offences such as tax-evasion, moonshining and jaywalking seemed to him to be pardonable, even typically American. What he could not tolerate was theft, because sooner or later theft meant *gold*.

Once he was in his casual clothes he liked to forget about gold, but on that particular afternoon it was not possible. He had just switched on the TV when the ball-game was abruptly replaced by an excited news-caster: *'We interrupt this programme to bring you a special news flash. Reports are just coming in that Fort Knox has been robbed. First reports indicate that a single raider wearing – uh, a platinum suit broke through the hitherto impenetrable security cordon, melting all obstacles with some kind of energy ray, and removed the entire contents of the U.S. Bullion Depository single-handed. At least 150 guards have been injured, some of them severely.'*

The normally impassive face of the TV announcer reflected the shock and amazement which was undoubtedly shared by his audience. *'Well, we'll certainly be coming back to you with more details of this incredible robbery as soon as they get through. – And yes, viewers, here's a further bulletin – reports are beginning to come in that the Bank of England in London and the French National Gold Reserve in Paris have also been raided. This is the most amazing thing that has ever happened! The Norwegian State Bank in Oslo . . . From New Delhi . . . reports are pouring in from all parts of the world of raids on national gold reserves. From Zurich, Switzerland, come reports of seventeen simultaneous raids on different banks, all of them aimed at safe deposit boxes apparently containing gold bullion. From Cape Town . . .'*

It's got to be a hoax, Captain Amazing told himself numbly. It was as if his worst nightmare was coming true. For the first time in his entire existence he felt weak, powerless . . .

Suddenly the door of the room disintegrated into matchwood, and as Captain Amazing hurled himself from his chair he found himself confronted by the

Chairman of the High Council of Sirius-D and four other council members.

'So! You are the Sirian renegade who calls himself Captain Amazing,' sneered the Chairman. 'Wretch, we are taking you home to Sirius-D to stand trial for betraying the ideals of your people.'

'You!' gasped Captain Amazing. 'It was you who committed all those robberies.'

'We had to do it to discredit you,' said the Chairman. 'For too long you have opposed yourself to all you are, to all our race stands for.'

'I never wanted to be Captain Amazing,' protested Captain Amazing, 'I just wanted to be an ordinary American. But I had to use my powers in self-defence . . .'

They ignored his cries of 'Gold is poison, *poison*! Keep away from it!' They ignored his struggles; the man who could stop a hurtling express train with one finger and who could throw a giant oil tanker into orbit was a mere boy in the hands of the five Sirian leaders. Faster than a rocket plane they whisked him across the Atlantic, across the coast of North Africa, and across five hundred miles of the Sahara Desert, till below them two Sirian spacecraft gleamed in the gathering dusk. As they descended Captain Amazing could see the burn marks where large numbers of other spacecraft had landed and already taken off.

There was no sign of life around the two parked spaceships. Captain Amazing noticed that the Chairman of the High Council seemed puzzled by this; doubtless he had expected a guard to be on duty. Captain Amazing could guess what had happened to the guard; there was a heavy concentration of gold rays in the area, indicating the presence of enough gold to kill every Sirian in the neighbourhood in less than an hour. He could see that his captors were already beginning to wilt; he himself, though partially immune after living so long on Earth, was beginning to feel nauseous.

'It's poison I tell you,' he said. 'It has absolutely no

effect on the Earthlings but it's fatal to us Sirians. That's why I've had to wage an unending war against gold thieves all over the world. If it wasn't for people trying to steal gold, most of it would be kept in underground stores where it couldn't harm us, and the rest would be distributed in minute quantities, in rings and bracelets, which are far too small to give off fatal doses of gold radiation. I had to stop villains transporting lethal quantities all over the place, without warning.'

His five captors were not listening. Already they were on the verge of sinking into coma. He hustled them into one of the spaceships and activated the time-launch-switch which would give him a minute to get clear before the vessel automatically launched itself. Then he activated the time-launch-switch on the other vessel. As the two spaceships lifted off in a swirl of smoke and sand, Captain Amazing breathed a sigh of relief. The atmosphere already seemed less charged with radiation. Nearly all the gold in the world was now safely on its way to Sirius-D.

He felt a short-lived regret for all his fellow Sirians who were, at that very moment, dying of gold ray poisoning on board the spaceships, and for all the other Sirians when the spaceships returned to their bases with their fatal loads. But then, he had always wanted to be an Earthling, not a Sirian, and now that nearly all of Earth's gold had gone, it would be much safer for him to live an ordinary, average, unheroic life, like any other ordinary, average, unheroic Earthling.

'Maybe I'll even be able to get married at last,' he said to himself as he headed for home.

The Awesome Menace of *The Polarizer*

by George Alec Effinger

This is New Haven, Connecticut. It is a city not without its large share of New England charm, not without its proud heritage dating from more than a century before the American Revolution, a city not without . . . fear!

New Haven has a large and beautiful central green, with its three white, steepled churches. The Elm City is the home of Yale University and the world-famous Peabody Museum. It is the home of Robert W. Hanson, whose fate is inextricably bound to that of Rod Marquand, who, in his secret guise of The Iguana, is in actuality a superpowered battler against crime and iniquity.

What strange destinies have drawn these two men, so disparate in their goals and accomplishments, together in a weird struggle against the massed forces of evil? Let us go back in time, back just a few days, to New York City, to the office of the principal of a great metropolitan high school . . .

'Rod, I'm going to send you to the dispensary, and then we'll send you home for the day. You're obviously in no condition to stay in school. While the nurse is looking at you, I'll call your parents and let them know that you're on your way. I wish you'd tell me what happened. You know, protecting whoever did this to you can only make things worse for yourself, and will end in the same thing happening to someone else. When it does, he may not get off as lightly as you.'

Young Rod Marquand, straight-A scholar and star athlete, nodded silently. He couldn't tell Principal Woodcotte the truth: that during the lunch recess he had intercepted a call by Safety Director Madison and had hurried to a location on the far West Side. There, on the lonely rooftop of the riverfront warehouse, he had battled his oldest enemy, The Polarizer, whom Rod had believed to be still safely salted away in a Federal penitentiary. The Polarizer had managed to develop a unique new weapon, an improvement on his earlier wrist-ionizer. Rod, The Iguana, had been defeated, although the Tactical Police Force arrived before The Polarizer could seriously injure him or, worse, remove his mask. After the battle, Rod returned to school to protect his normal identity. But he was wounded badly on the face and body, and still reeling from the effects of The Polarizer's de-molecularizer.

'Yes, sir. It was only some envious members of that Ethnic Group, out for some fun at my expense. I'm positive that they wouldn't bother someone less popular. Thank you for letting me go home; I don't feel very well right now. But when you talk to my parents, please don't tell them how badly I feel. They're both aged and infirm, and the worry might be bad for their health.'

'Rod, you're amazing. You've just been roughed-up by a gang of young hoods, and you're concerned only with your parents' feelings. I certainly wish more of my students here were like you.'

'May I go now, sir?'

'Certainly, Rod. Go down to see the nurse and she'll give you the yellow slip to go home. Here, let me write you a hall pass.'

Hanson rode his bicycle down the hill from the Chem Lab. It had rained during the afternoon and he discovered that his hand brakes wouldn't work. He built speed down the long hill, shooting past the Pregnant Oyster and through the light at Grove Street. He zipped around the corner and coasted by the cemetery.

He pedalled on for several blocks until he came to the driveway of his apartment building. He parked the bike in the back, taking his lab manual and notebook out of the basket. They were spotted with water, soaked in stripes from the wet wire pannier.

Hanson walked around to the front of the building,

in order to check his mailbox. There wasn't any mail, but he did see a small, shiny brass plaque screwed to the wall of the entry hall. He was certain that he had never seen one there before. It read:

THIS BUILDING
houses the apartment used by
ROBERT WAYNE HANSON
during his years at
Yale University
1966–1970

Hanson laughed to himself. 'Those bastards at YBC, I'll bet,' he thought. The idea struck him as pretty funny, although the engraved plaque must have cost someone a good bit. He took out his handkerchief and polished the metal. Still smiling, he went down the corridor to his rooms.

Inside, he put his books on his desk and stretched out on the couch. He had nothing to do until dinner-time, and he felt like taking a nap. He was startled to see that the Miro print that he had put on the living room wall above the couch was missing. In its place was another brass plaque, much larger than the other. This one said:

THIS ROOM
was the home of
ROBERT WAYNE HANSON
during the years
1966–1970

Hanson didn't laugh. The concept of the joke still amused him, but he was a little upset that someone had come into his apartment without his permission, removed his favourite print, and permanently mounted a large and altogether unattractive sign on his wall.

'That goddamn Benarcek and his preppie sense of humour. There'll probably be pig entrails in the bathtub.' Hanson frowned and closed his eyes. He would put off thinking about the Miro print until he had a chance to talk to Justin and the rest of the clowns at the radio station.

Rod worried all the way home on the subway. The Polarizer had beaten him badly, and, though the Crimemaster had been fooled by Rod's display of sheer will-power, Rod knew that he had nearly been killed. Only the fact that The Iguana's electromagnetic web-rope had jammed the de-molecularizer in time had saved Rod's life. But Rod was certain that The Polarizer would not be satisfied with a private victory; even now the King of Evil would be plotting an even more ignominious and public end of The Iguana. Rod was sure that an invitation to the trap would not be long in coming.

There was only one thing to do. He had to get help from someone. But who? Who was the leading physicist in the country? And, moreover, could Rod trust him with the secret of his dual identity? He couldn't face The Polarizer again without something to neutralize the effects of the Valence Wizard's uncanny weapons.

'Fortunately,' Rod thought, 'spring vacation begins tomorrow. I can get help and be back before school starts again. Also, fortunately, Dad is aware of my secret. He can make up some excuse for my absence that will satisfy Mom and the guys.' Mr Marquand had dramatically discovered Rod's concealed role as The Iguana several weeks previously. Rod had just been severely beaten by Kobol, the cybernetic man-thing programmed to pulverize Manhattan by Diabor The Devastator. Mr Marquand came upon his son's twisted and inert body by accident that evening, as he walked along Bleeker Street. Many other passers-by had avoided the boy, but Mr Marquand knelt and lifted off the fearsome mask. He gasped when he recognized his son, and, hailing a cab, took him home. He hid the costume of The Iguana to protect the already shattered nerves of his wife. Soon Rod's athletic young body recovered completely, in time to defeat Kobol and wreck the insane plans of Diabor The Devastator.

Safe in his family's Chelsea apartment, Rod studied the piles of scientific journals to which he subscribed. After much deliberation, he came to the conclusion that there was only one man who could possibly aid him in his effort to save humanity from the megalomaniac scheme of The Polarizer: Dr Waters, head of the plasmonics department at Ivy University. Rod called the Port Authority information number, and prepared for his trip to New Aulis in the morning.

Spring vacation! Hanson was grateful down through his very bones. He hadn't needed a vacation this much in years. He had two long papers to write, but he already had them pretty well thought out, so that he could spend the time just lying around his parents' home in Cleveland.

His father met him at Hopkins Airport, asking him the same questions as always: how was he getting along, did he need anything, had he knocked up any Vassar girls ha ha. His mother would ask him about the food, of course. Everything was always the same, which is the reason that he wanted to come home for the rest.

Everything was always the same, except for the bronze inscription bolted to the porch of the house on E. 147th Street. Hanson dropped his suitcase when he saw it. He walked up to the porch and read it:

THIS HOUSE
was the birthplace of
ROBERT WAYNE HANSON
November 15, 1947
* * *
Marker donated by
The Cleveland Historical Society

'What's this, Dad? How long has this been here?'

'I don't know, Bobby. I never saw it before.'

Hanson was getting confused. This was a bit too much for a silly joke by some of the guys at school. This unsightly testimonial on the front of his parents' house looked very expensive; when could it have been put there? Neither of his parents had ever seen it before, and were sure that no one had put it there that morning. Hanson idly wondered if there were a little marker now in the delivery room at St Ann's Hospital.

On a whim he called the Cleveland Historical Society. A female voice answered his questions, and transferred him to the Bureau of Landmarks and Monuments. A helpful clerk in the department informed him that the plaque had been put on the house over six years ago.

'But I was only twelve years old then,' protested Hanson.

'Yes, sir. Our records show that the house at that address was declared a local landmark, and funds were appropriated for the plaque.'

'In the first place, we've lived there for over twenty years, and we've never seen that thing before. And even if it were there, which is impossible, why would the Historical Society put up markers for me?'

'I don't understand, I'm afraid. We have the records right here in our files. You must have overlooked the plaque all this time. Perhaps it was behind a bush which you've recently removed.'

'But it's for me! *I'm* Robert W. Hanson, and I haven't *done* anything!'

'What was that?'

'I said, *I'm* Robert Hanson.'

The voice sounded annoyed and impatient. 'I see. A joke. You're Robert Wayne Hanson. And I'm Margaret Chase Smith. Good afternoon.'

'Mr Marquand?'

'Yes, sir?'

'I'm Dr Waters. I hope your trip out from New York was pleasant.'

'Yes, sir. Very much so. I caught up on some thin-film abstracts that I've been wanting to get to. I'd like to thank you for taking time out to see me. You have no idea how serious my problem is.'

The physicist, surprisingly young and athletic for one of his intellectual attainments, smiled. 'I'm always glad to help along a struggling scholar. Are you planning to apply to old Ivy?'

'Oh, I've already been accepted by Yale, Harvard, and Princeton,' said Rod shyly, 'but I think that I'm going to turn them all down and go to Cambridge. I'll get to do some travelling that way, too.'

'Very interesting. Now, as to your problem . . .'

Rod nodded, rising and coming closer to Dr Waters' desk.

'I must be sure, first of all,' he said, 'it is vital that we are completely alone. Is there any way for anyone to overhear our conversation?'

Dr Waters looked amused. 'This is somewhat more melodramatic than the usual confrontation with undergraduates. But, all right, just a moment.' He pressed a button on the intercom on his desk. 'Miss Clement, please see that we're not interrupted for any reason. Thank you.'

'Fine,' said Rod. 'Now you will understand my need for secrecy. First, I must reveal to you that I am, in actuality, The Iguana.'

'What!' exclaimed Dr Waters. 'You! A mere lad! If what you say is true, I'm utterly amazed. From the motion pictures I had estimated that The Iguana must be a marvellously trained adult with years of academic and athletic experience behind him.'

Rod opened his suitcase, removing his brightly coloured costume. 'I anticipated your doubts; they're quite reasonable, actually. Watch.' He uncoiled his electromagnetic webrope; then he pointed at a bird flying past Dr Waters' open window. Rod threw the weighted end of the webrope expertly, catching the helpless bird within the coils. He pulled the bird into the room, disconnected the webrope, and freed the bird once more.

'Yes,' said Dr Waters, 'I can see that you are, indeed, the famous Iguana. You have my respect, young man, although I don't understand why you insist on tackling such dangerous assignments instead of contenting yourself with more normal pursuits.'

Rod just smiled, folding the webrope compactly into its place in his costume's belt.

'And I don't understand why you decided to reveal your identity to me. That could have been a dangerous move.'

'I looked into your background first,' Rod said. 'You are the pre-eminent and most respected man in your field, and I need someone of your calibre to advise me.'

'I see,' said Dr Waters, sitting back and making a steeple of his two forefingers. 'I am, of course, flattered. But, do go on with your story.'

'Yes, sir. I must explain to you how my webrope works. A few months ago I stumbled onto the basic principles of magnetism, the subatomic binding force which holds all things together. Of course, as you know, magnetism is an oversimplified term to use to describe the actual mysterious play of electrical forces within the atom. But, in any event, I have learned how it is possible to align the electrons of the surface shells of *any* group of atoms, so that the molecule will be irresistibly and permanently attracted to the magnetic centre. This centre is, of course, my webrope. It is activated by a certain frequency of radio waves transmitted by this sending device on my belt. When it is operating, the webrope will adhere with all the strength of the limitless power of the atom to whatever it touches. When I shut off the transmitter, the webrope drops off, and the object falls loose, totally unharmed.'

'That's utterly fantastic!' cried Dr Waters. 'What a boon to mankind that discovery will be when you decide to publish it.'

'Yes,' said Rod sombrely. 'Since the initial breakthrough, I have refined the mechanism even further. These controls over here permit me to throw the web-rope as a thin but incredibly strong line, or as an inescapable net, as I choose. I have employed the same principles in these patches on my gloves and boots, so that I may, with some difficulty, climb vertical walls and stand upon ceilings.'

'And, with all this, you need me? That seems unlikely.'

'You are being modest,' said Rod. 'I am faced with a desperate battle, the most dangerous since the beginning of my career as a defender of Freedom. I must face The Polarizer, who, since our last encounter, has developed a weapon that I am powerless to analyze, much less defeat. Your resources here, in the Department of Plasmonics, and your own superior knowledge, may be all that stands between civilization as we know it and abject slavery under that maniacal monster, The Polarizer.'

The professor rose from his desk, his face flushed and his voice shaking with rage. ' "Maniac"?! "Monster", am I? Because I recognize my manifest destiny, my fate, my *right* to rule the world? I, Dr Bertram Waters, The Polarizer, I *will* rule, for the simple reason that no one can stop me!' He laughed, pushing back his chair. He came around his desk, but Rod had already reached for his webrope. The Polarizer shook his head.

'Flee, you idiot. Flee before I de-molecularize you on the spot. Now we both know each other's true identities; but it will do you no good at all, while I can play with you through the avenue of those whom you are so weak as to love! Go! We shall meet again soon – for the final time!'

Rod fumbled his suitcase closed, knowing that he was helplessly off-guard. He hurried from the office with the demented laughter of The Polarizer ringing in his ears. He had nowhere else to turn; the regular law-enforcement authorities were no match at all for The

Polarizer's overwhelming might. He knew that he must defeat the madman himself.

Bob Hanson walked through the garden, along the winding paths that he had known so well as a child. At the far end of the garden was the goldfish pond. He had always loved the pool; it had been the first place that he had ever seen live fish. When he had first started school he used to climb up on the stone pedestal and look into the water. His mother had told him that the bits of yellow and orange were the fish; the sudden splashes he knew to be frogs. In those days the garden and the pond were places warm with their own childhood holiness, and the feeling still hung over them, so that this visit, his first in several years, took on the significance of a pilgrimage.

Hanson paused to read the familiar words on the stone pedestal. The words were cast on a bronze slab, and told of the deaths by fire of scores of children and teachers early in the century. The new school that had been built on the site had been named Memorial, and this is where Hanson had begun his education.

The pedestal was larger than it had been years ago, but the plaque was still stuck on low, so that he could hardly read it without stooping. Above it was another that said:

Memorial School
ROBERT W. HANSON
attended this school and doubtless
formulated here those ideals
which guided his later career
* * *
'We Must All Make Sacrifices'
* * *
Plaque presented by the
Cleveland Board of Education

Hanson frowned, his mind moving rapidly to no purpose, like a rat in a solutionless maze. It had been nine years since he had graduated from the elementary school; he saw that a new wing had been added. He went up the front steps and, although the children were on vacation, the doors were open and the teachers appeared to be at work. He walked through the dim, draughty halls, remembering how the rooms had seemed to him then. He marvelled at the change in scale: the auditorium used to seem so immense!

Here was Room 111. Old Miss Hatterley, third grade. Miss Hatterley had taught him about Sacagawea and how to do book reports. She had probably already retired. In the room, of course, was a bronze marker proclaiming that Robert Wayne Hanson had sat in one of these tiny chairs and learned to spell.

Room 216. Mrs Loveness. He had had a secret crush on her when he was nine years old. Fractions and Peru. Another plaque on the wall.

'Excuse me, but there's not supposed to be anyone but teachers here today. If you're visiting, you can check in at the principal's office.'

'I'm sorry,' said Hanson, a bit startled. 'I used to go to school here. I'm home from college this week and I thought I'd look around.'

'I see,' said the teacher, a young woman not much older than Hanson himself. 'I went here, too. Perhaps we were here at the same time. I'm Leigh Leonard, kindergarten and first grade.'

Hanson took her hand and smiled. 'I'm Bob Hanson. I'm a senior at Yale.'

Miss Leonard looked at him strangely. '*The* Robert Hanson went to this school, too, you know. And *he* went to Yale. What a funny coincidence.'

'*The* Robert Hanson? You know, until a short while ago I had always thought of myself as *the* Robert Hanson. I've never heard of any other.'

The young teacher was faintly shocked. 'That is unusual. After all, you went to school here. This *is* Robert W. Hanson Memorial School. It was nice meeting you,

Mr., er, Hanson. If you want to look around any more, perhaps you'd better see Mr Ladely in his office on the first floor.'

Hanson nodded absently. He was beginning to get frightened. *Robert W. Hanson Memorial School?*

Rod Marquand was half-crazed with fear. How could he protect all of his friends and relatives against the senseless attacks of the murderous Polarizer? There were too many people, too many opportunities. The only thing to do was to meet The Polarizer first, and defeat him. Rod's superior intellect had enabled him to beat enemy after enemy, each aided by superscientific gadgetry and superhuman powers. But none of them posed the threat represented by The Polarizer.

And the mad Doctor Waters could follow his every move, choosing Rod's unguarded moments for his attack.

Rod worked for hours on end, not stopping for food or rest. His father told Rod's friends and his mother that he had a great deal of schoolwork to make up, but even Mr Marquand did not realize the extent of the danger. Rod sweated and cursed over the problem, but at last, nearing the point of exhaustion, he found an answer.

The Interstitial Molecular Insulationizer.

This electromagnetic device would serve to insulate the single-molecule surface layers of all objects within its effective operating radius. Thus, theoretically, The Polarizer's ionizing de-molecularizer would not be able to penetrate the zone of protection, and the weapon's awesome potential for destruction would be nullified.

Just as Rod was putting the final chromium touches to his jury-rigged working model, his father ran into his workroom.

'Rod! The Polarizer has jammed all radio and television networks and is broadcasting a message. He is challenging you to a battle-to-the-death under The

Clock at the Biltmore. You can't meet him, son! He sounds serious!'

Rod gazed at his father tiredly. 'He is, Dad. This is it, I'm afraid. This is a battle that is larger than you can know. This is a battle to save everything that we've worked for since our ancestors left their trees to the apes. But I think I have it.' He showed the machine to his father.

'What is it, son?'

'An electromagnetic Interstitial Molecular Insulationizer. Now, how do I get in touch with The Polarizer.'

His father frowned. 'He doesn't want an answer, fearing that he may be tricked. He just expects you to show up at noon tomorrow.'

'All right,' said Rod resolutely, 'then noon it will be. Wake me at eleven.'

'I see you brought one of your little Radio Shack toys,' said The Polarizer with a sneer. 'I suppose you think that piece of junk will save your scaly hide.'

'Yes,' said The Iguana sternly, 'and if you don't surrender now, and agree to return to prison to finish out your sentence, I'll be forced to use it.'

'I don't think so!' laughed the Fiend of Crime, firing a burst from his wrist-ionizer at Rod's machine. The IMI began to haze over with a rainbow aura of free ions, and before it could be activated the Insulationizer was destroyed.

'Damn it,' growled Rod. He knew that now he was in for a tough time.

Just then, fortunately for him, a man walked into the lobby of the New Biltmore, standing between the two costumed duellers, apparently unaware of the significance of the combat.

'I'm supposed to meet this cheese from Smith here,' said the intruder. 'You haven't seen her, have you?'

'Hanson!' screamed The Polarizer. 'How did you get here? Get out! Get out of here before you're hurt! I worked too hard, for too many years for you to lose it for me now.'

Rod took advantage of the interruption to do some quick thinking. The de-molecularizer could easily nullify the effects of The Iguana's webrope *under normal circumstances.* 'If only . . . I can . . . jam . . . the circuit-breakers . . . overload . . . it might be enough . . .'

Rod aimed the webrope well. He flung it out, covering The Polarizer's wrist-ionizers and the de-molecularizer as well. The Polarizer grinned evilly. 'That didn't help you before, and it won't help you now,' he said.

Meanwhile, Hanson fell back, astonished, hiding behind a stuffed plush couch.

Rod held the circuitbreakers in place. Oblivious to the painful current that ran through his fingers. The weapons of the two masked men sparked under the strains put upon them. A weird, low humming filled the room.

'My God, what's that?' thought Rod. 'It doesn't seem to be my circuitry. Perhaps The Polarizer is in more trouble than he thought.' The Iguana glanced at his adversary. The Polarizer's face was hidden to a large extent by his grotesque mask, but Rod could see the frown of concentration and concern.

The humming sound grew louder.

'It's him!' shouted The Polarizer. 'It's Hanson! Turn it off! I didn't keep his brain alive for fifteen years to have it end like this! Turn it off before—'

'Aaarrgghh!' Rod was thrown back against the wall of the lobby by a tremendous explosion. He hit the wall heavily, hurting his shoulder and falling to the floor. He couldn't focus his eyes through the smoke, and he lost consciousness.

When he awoke, he saw that the hotel lobby was entirely demolished. The body of Hanson was lying in bits all over the ruined carpet. No sign of The Polarizer could be seen. Apparently he had been buried under the tons of rubble. Rod examined himself gingerly. His uniform had been tattered by the blast, but outside of some very painful burns and bruises, he seemed to be uninjured. He heard the sounds of footsteps – no doubt the police. He decided to leave the mopping up to them, and fled the scene.

'How do you feel?' asked his father.

'All right, I guess. Relieved, too, that the threat of The Polarizer is finished for good. Say, what's wrong with Mom?' Mrs Marquand was sprawled on the family's living room floor, evidently unconscious.

'You see, the police decided to televise the entire conflict. We watched it all, right there on Channel 9. After the explosion, when they moved in for a close-up of you, we saw that your mask had been torn off. Your mother recognized you then. She went into a state of shock, I believe. We both thought that you were dead.'

'Well, I'm all right now,' said Rod, 'but don't you think that we ought to call an ambulance for Mom?'

'Good thinking, son. But tell me, what exactly happened?'

'I think that I have a pretty clear picture. That young man that interrupted us—'

'Hanson?' asked his father, dialling the phone.

'Yes. He wasn't a real human being.'

'*What?* Not a real person? Why, how could that be?'

'He was an MIS, or Modular Identity Synthecator. He was, in other words, an android.'

'Android?'

'Right, Dad. Like a robot, only more life-like. The Polarizer had built a perfect replica of a human being, and housed within it an actual, living human brain.'

'The brain of Robert W. Hanson!'

'Exactly. The Polarizer – who was, incidentally, Dr Waters of the famous Ivy Plasmonics Laboratory – had built the android and controlled him through Hanson's brain, feeding the mind with a consistent but false set of surrogate memories. Apparently Hanson was to play a part in The Polarizer's scheme of world conquest. It is merely a strange coincidence that the android happened by at just that time.'

'It *is* ironic, at that. The Polarizer, defeated by his own demonic creation,' said Mr Marquand, holding the limp form of his wife.

'It just occurred to me that Dr Waters may have been the very person who stole Robert Hanson's body from the catafalque, as the corpse rested in state fifteen years ago. That would fit in with The Polarizer's last comments. What a genius, to have kept the brain alive all that time. If only he had turned that genius to work for the cause of justice.'

'Yes,' said Mr Marquand. 'But, what caused the explosion?'

'I believe I have the answer. As I was building up the power in my belt-transformer, the frequency from the transmitter shifted just slightly. It's possible that the frequency was precisely that which could cause a feedback reaction in the sensitive system of the MIS; thus, the android's own power supply shorted and caused the whole thing to explode.'

'How fortunate for all of us.'

'Yes,' agreed Rod solemnly. 'And now, I guess my career as The Iguana has ended at the same time as that of The Polarizer.'

'Yes, son. And I can't say that I'm sorry. It's good to have you back.'

'It's good to *be* back, Dad,' said Rod, peeking through the blinds to see if the ambulance had arrived yet.

Satyr-Man

by John A. Keel

'Harry,' Mildred Chromik rasped lovingly, looking at her husband through the gleaming V of her knitting needles. 'Turn the television down. I think those new people next door are having another fight.'

'Fer Pete's sake, Millie,' Harry Chromik grumbled, his eyes fixed on the hypnotic glass rectangle. 'I bin waitin' all week to see this show.'

'Please, Harry. Am I asking too much? Do I ever ask for much?' She glared at her husband, her lips pursed. 'Do I ever ask for a new coat like Missus Travaski has got? Do I ever . . .'

'All right, all right!' Harry leaned forward and lowered the volume on the television set. 'How's that? Can you hear better now?'

Mildred Chromik cocked her head, her sharp ears picking up the distant sound of screams and shouting.

'You know somthin', Harry? Those sounds aren't coming from next door. They're comin' from the street.'

Harry groaned and turned his head, listening to the sounds.

'I think you're right,' he agreed. 'Sounds like somebody gettin' killed out there.'

'Maybe you'd better take a look, Harry,' Mildred suggested firmly.

'Fer Pete's sake,' he mumbled as he got out of his easy chair – the only piece of furniture that had come with their ninety-two-dollar living-room set that he could stand. He put his can of beer on the plastic top of a nearby table and shuffled in his bare feet to the window. He opened the window and looked out briefly. The sounds grew louder.

'No . . . No!' a man screamed.

'Take that . . . and that . . . and that!' another voice roared, the words interspersed with dull thuds.

POW!!! CLUNK!!!

Harry frowned and muttered to himself. He closed the window and padded back to his chair.

'Waited all week to see this show,' he muttered under his breath. The sounds outside continued.

'Well, Harry?' Mildred asked. 'What was it?'

'I was right,' he growled, his eyes again fixed on the TV screen. 'Somebody's gettin' killed out there.'

'Oh.' Mildred returned to her knitting. After a few stitches she spoke again. 'Maybe we oughta call the police or something.'

'Are you out of your skull, Millie?' Harry snapped. He picked up his can of beer. 'It's none of our damned business.'

'But maybe somebody is gettin' hurt.'

'No doubt about it,' Harry mumbled, concentrating on the TV programme. 'He's gettin' the hell beat out of him.'

'That's a shame.' Mildred shook her head sympathetically. 'Gettin' so it ain't safe to walk the streets at night anymore. Somebody ought to do something.' She stitched away sadly. 'They sure are makin' a lot of noise.'

'They sure are,' Harry grunted as he turned the volume back up.

The TV announcer's voice was droning on: 'And now we continue with the second half of our National Good Neighbour Test . . .'

Down in the street below the Chromiks' window two burly thugs with large muscles and small brows were methodically hammering their fists against the delicate flesh of a small, elderly man in a neat blue serge suit. His horn-rimmed glasses lay on the sidewalk and the two men were tromping on them as they took turns trying to rearrange his features. The little man was not taking this punishment with much grace. He was, in fact, rather hysterical.

'Lousy cheapskate,' one of the hoodlums complained as he planted his fist in the little man's stomach. 'Only got a dollar and forty cents on you, huh?'

'Please,' the little man gasped as he doubled over. 'I'll go home and get more.'

'Getting so there's nobody worth rolling in this rotten neighbourhood,' the other man observed as he delivered a well-placed rabbit punch. The little man fell forward on his face. The first thug grabbed him by the back of his collar and lifted him like a sack of wet laundry.

'All this trouble for a miserable dollar and forty cents! We oughta break every bone in your head!'

The little man moaned miserably.

Suddenly, out of the darkness there came the powerful roar of a souped-up motor scooter.

VAROOOM!

Both muggers snapped their heads up, their pig-eyes clouding with sudden fear. A heavy, streamlined motor scooter appeared at the end of the street, darting toward them through the soft haze of the inadequate lights.

'It's *him*!' they cried in unison, releasing the little man.

'Let's get out of here!' one of the thugs exclaimed. He started to run, closely followed by his comrade in crime. But their sturdy legs were no match for the pounding pistons of the world's fastest motor scooter. Before they had taken five steps the scooter was upon them and the masked man sitting astride it, cape flapping in the wind, leaped through the air toward them. His sinewy arms reached out and encircled the two muggers like bands of steel. Meanwhile, his motor scooter careened wildly up the street and came to rest against a pile of garbage cans with a loud clatter.

'We didn't do nothin',' one of the thugs managed to cry before the masked man brought his head in sharp contact with the head of his companion. There was a sickening CRUNCH and both toughs found instant sleep. Slinging one over each shoulder, the masked man turned with a flourish, his cape swirling behind him, and walked over to the little man who was struggling into an upright position.

'Don't hit me anymore,' the little man pleaded, looking up with glazed and frightened eyes, seeing only the mask on the face before him.

'I'm not going to hit you,' the masked man said gently, in a deep and resonant voice. 'My mission is to protect honest citizens like yourself from vermin such as this.' With those words he threw the two muggers to the pavement contemptuously. 'Are you hurt badly?'

'I think all my teeth have been knocked out and I may have a couple of broken ribs,' the little man answered, wincing as he tried to move.

'Hmmm . . . that's unfortunate,' the masked man said sympathetically. 'But I know a good dentist. It is too bad that I didn't get here sooner though.' He looked up at the buildings along the street. There were rows of lighted windows with pale faces peering out of them. 'Will one of you good people call an ambulance?' he shouted.

All the windows slammed shut and the lights flicked out.

'Funny thing,' the masked man began thoughtfully. 'That always happens. Maybe people are afraid of my costume.'

'You . . . you do have an unusual tailor,' the little man noted as he studied his rescuer. The masked man was wearing dark velvet leotards and a tight-fitting green sweat shirt made of the finest velour. His long red cape was made of imported silk, and he was shod in expensive English boots. His head was encased in a contoured helmet made of jet-age plastic, obviously bulletproof. Most of his face was hidden behind a sinister mask designed to strike terror in the hearts of evildoers. Altogether, he was an imposing figure surrounded by an aura of strength and dignity.

'I would have come sooner,' he apologized. 'But I didn't know this was happening. Lucky thing I happened to be passing by.'

'I'm grateful . . . but maybe if you'd gotten here sooner I could have saved a couple of teeth.' The little man struggled to his feet and brushed himself off. 'Are you on your way to a masquerade party?'

'No.' The masked man sounded insulted. 'These are my working clothes.'

'Oh. I won't ask you what your job is.' The little man smiled wanly, his mouth a chasm. 'I'm an archaeologist. Just came back from Egypt.' He pulled out a business card and handed it to his benefactor.

'Ahaha,' said the masked man. 'Perhaps this explains it. You are pro-Egyptian and this is a Jewish neighbourhood.'

'I'm not "pro" anything. I was just on my way to visit my beautiful daughter when these two monsters jumped me.'

'Beautiful daughter, huh?' The masked man's mouth became a tight line and he licked his lips slightly. 'I forgot for a moment . . . all scientists have beautiful daughters.' He took the little man gently by the arm. 'Perhaps I can take you to her on my motor scooter.'

The little man held back fearfully.

'Is . . . is it safe to ride a motor scooter with broken ribs?'

'Of course. My scooter has hydraulic springs and counter-tension bars.'

The masked man led the bruised and battered victim to the motor scooter and helped him onto it.

'We'll be there in a trice,' he said reassuringly. A police siren wailed in the distance. 'Hmmm . . . sounds as if some good citizen has finally called the police. They'll take care of those two hoodlums.'

'Maybe I should stick around,' the little man said nervously.

'Forget it. Do you want to have to fill out all those forms and things? Let's go to your beautiful daughter so she can minister to your wounds.'

The scooter roared to life and they plunged down the street, the masked man's cape lashing into the little man's face as he clung precariously to the rear of the machine. A police car appeared at the other end of the street and sped toward the scene of the crime. A man in his undershirt ran out into the street and pointed in the direction of the disappearing motor scooter.

'After them, officers!' he cried. 'They knocked over my garbage cans!'

The police car sped away as the two thugs sat up on the sidewalk, shaking their heads groggily. They got to their feet and staggered down the street.

Above, Mildred Chromik stood by her window gazing down into the darkness.

'Get away from the window, Millie,' Harry ordered. 'Do you want the cops to see you and think you were a witness or something?'

'Harry, I just saw the damndest thing. Some nut in his long johns came up on a motor scooter and . . .'

'Lousy beatniks,' Harry grumbled, staring at his TV. 'Gettin' so an honest man can't get a little relaxation around here.'

'But Harry . . . he wasn't a beatnik. He was wearing a mask and a funny cape.' She returned to her chair and picked up her knitting thoughtfully. 'I wonder who he was? I wonder what he was doing here in Brooklyn?'

'The whole damned neighbourhood has gone to pot,' Harry muttered, swigging from his can of beer and scratching himself.

Bonita Grant sighed contentedly, stretching her voluptuous body across the rumpled bed like a self-satisfied cat. The muscular man on the bed beside her stirred slightly and looked at her, a pleased smile playing about the corners of his lips. She raised her hand and tenderly touched the mask that covered half his face.

'Do you always wear your jet-age plastic mask in bed?' she asked with wonder.

'Always,' he replied laconically.

'But I can't kiss your ears,' she pouted. She leaned over his prostrate form and pressed her magnificently rounded breasts against his bare chest. He encircled her slender waist with his arm and pulled her closer, patting her gently on her plump bottom.

'There are other places for you to kiss,' he suggested. His deep, rumbling voice sent a shiver through her.

'I know,' she laughed. 'But I happen to have an ear fetish.'

'Hmmm,' he hmmed. 'It seems to me I've read about such a fetish somewhere. It's peculiar to the natives of the South Seas. It was described in great detail in a book called, *Love South of Pago-Pago*.'

'I know, silly. I wrote it.' She explored the nape of his neck with her tongue.

'You wrote it!' He looked at her in surprise. 'Then your name must be Bonita Grant . . . the famous sexologist!'

'That's right.'

'Aha. Now everything is becoming crystal clear,' he mused thoughtfully. 'That explains everything.'

'Everything? It doesn't explain why you insist on wearing this silly mask. What kind of fetish is that?'

'I must hide my real identity,' he explained, trembling slightly as her tongue discovered certain sensitive nerves. 'It's the only way I can remain effective in my unending war against crime. This mask strikes fear into the hearts of evildoers.' He giggled as her tongue found a new target.

'Well, I find it fascinating,' she admitted. Her fingers stroked the hairs on his manly chest. 'And I'm so grateful to you for rescuing my father from those villainous footpads.'

'It was all in a night's work,' he said modestly.

'Nevertheless, I wish there were some way I could repay you.'

'You have repaid me manyfold in the last two hours.' He slapped her playfully. She responded by crushing herself closer to him and kissing him passionately on the lips. He pushed her away, kindly but firmly.

'Suppose your father should wake up in the other room?' he murmured.

'I gave him a strong sedative after I tended his wounds. He'll probably sleep until noon. Poor dear,' she whispered. 'He's had a terrible experience. In fact, bad luck has been dogging him ever since he was cursed by that mummy in Egypt.'

'Your father has been cursed by a mummy?' he mumbled as she raised herself and her swollen breasts inched toward his mouth.

'Didn't you know? Dad is Professor Gilroy Grant, the archaeologist. He opened . . .' She faltered, gasping as he kissed her hardening red nipples. 'He . . . he opened . . . the tomb of King Theops . . . There was a curse on it . . . Two . . . two of his colleagues have died horrible deaths since.'

'Hmmm . . . very interesting . . .' he managed to mutter.

'This jet-age plastic is cold against my skin,' she complained. 'I do wish you would take it off.'

'Never,' he grunted. He pushed her away and, with a single, well-practised movement, flipped her over on her back. 'For all I know, you may be an evildoer yourself.'

'Don't be absurd.' She smiled wantonly at him.

'Do you realize,' he began seriously, 'that in the last two hours you have broken twenty-two different laws. You have committed unnatural acts . . . out of wedlock.'

'So have you.' She looked away demurely.

'I know . . . I know,' he sighed. 'And don't think my conscience isn't bothering me.'

She laughed lightly and reached for him.

'You silly boy . . . I'm doing this as research for my new book, – *The Round-heels Syndrome*.'

'Indeed!' He looked slightly hurt. 'Well, that doesn't excuse me.' He casually caressed her creamy skin, inwardly reflecting on her perfection. She was a splendidly proportioned woman in her middle twenties. Her hair was a rich blonde. Naturally blonde, he noted with satisfaction. And her face had the sculpted beauty of a Grecian statue.

It had somehow seemed quite natural for them to be like this, he thought to himself as he reviewed recent events. She had been shocked and frightened when she first opened the door of her modest flat and found him standing there holding her fractured father in his arms. But she quickly sensed his innate goodness and enlisted his help in binding Professor Grant's caved-in ribs and nursing his numerous contusions. After the Professor had drifted off into welcome sleep she had made some coffee and slipped into something comfortable – a pair of transparent baby-doll pyjamas which revealed all of her considerable charms. No hero, no matter how stalwart, could resist such a display of pulchritude, and our hero, being no exception, soon found himself asserting his masculinity. He had asserted that masculinity several times since. And had not yet plumbed the bottom of this well of pleasure.

Her soft voice interrupted his reveries. 'Do you have a name?'

'Beg pardon,' he said dreamily.

'A name,' she repeated. 'I thought all of the men who ran around in capes and things had some sort of fancy names. What's yours?'

'That's a problem,' he said shyly, continuing his caresses. 'I've given it a lot of thought . . . but all of the good names have been taken. Like Batman, Superman, the Hulk . . . Of course, the criminal element in this city have all kinds of names for me. None of which I dare mention.'

'Hmmm,' she pondered, quivering slightly beneath his firm but gentle touch. 'That is . . . a problem.'

He kissed her soundly and held her in a tight embrace. Her soft body undulated invitingly against him. He felt new excitement gripping him. His body ached to revisit the site of its earlier conquest. She sensed the savage return of strength to his loins and her eyes widened with delight and wonder.

'I have it!' she cried.

'Not yet,' he said flatly. 'But you will.'

'Not that, silly, I have a name for you. A perfect name.'

'You have?' He paused in his manipulations and looked at her with interest. 'Will it strike fear in the hearts of all evildoers?'

'I guarantee it. It's the name of a mythical beast . . .' She closed her eyes, her ripe lips parting as she felt his pulsing flesh against hers. 'A . . . a beast with horns . . . with an . . . insatiable . . . sexual . . . appetite . . . a . . .'

'A horny beast, huh?' he grunted, poised for a sexual *coup de grace*.

'A satyr*,' she moaned in warm anticipation. 'Call . . . call yourself . . . Satyr-Man . . .'

'Satyr-Man . . . Satyr-Man . . .' He rolled the word over on his tongue as he thrust home. 'I like it!'

'So . . . so do I . . .' she groaned, her body meeting his, squirming with lust and hunger. 'Satyr-Man . . . part beast . . . part man . . . part . . .'

Entwined around each other, gasping and moaning in mutual delight, they celebrated the Fourth of July early.

'Damn this jet-age plastic mask,' she mumbled once and once only.

Satyr-Man rose early the next morning and carefully

*Rhymes with mate her.

donned his costume. Bonita was still sound asleep, coiled in lovely dishabille on the battlefield of the bed. He tiptoed around the room, picking up his scattered garments and slipping into them. Then he opened the door and walked into the bedroom where Professor Grant was sprawled on the Foamland sofa with a volume of the Kinsey Report serving as his pillow. Satyr-Man smiled benevolently down at him. Suddenly his highly trained nostrils twitched. Could it be? Yes . . . it was the unmistakable smell of a burning fuse. He looked around the room quickly and in the semi-darkness he perceived a long, flat object sticking under the door.

Without a moment's hesitation he rushed over to it, picked it up, and ran into the bathroom. Hastily he filled the bathtub with water and immersed the long, thin bomb. Then, rubbing his hands together with satisfaction, he walked back into the living room.

Bonita stood there, her eyes swollen with sleep. She was wearing the top of her baby-doll pyjamas and had a bewildered expression on her face.

'I heard the water running,' she mumbled sleepily.

'I was just disposing of a devilish bomb,' Satyr-Man said matter-of-factly.

'A bomb?'

'Yes – a very clever machine of destruction, designed so that it could be slipped under the door,' he explained.

'But who on earth would want to slip a bomb under my door?'

'A jilted suitor, perhaps,' Satyr-Man suggested. 'Or maybe you forgot to tip the janitor last Christmas.'

'No, I can't think of anybody who . . .' she began thoughtfully.

'Wait . . . I just realized . . .' he interjected brightly. 'Only one man in this city is capable of designing such a bomb. A warped ex-pharmacist turned mad scientist, named Irving Glasfogel. Once he was an honest citizen but vicious criminals convinced him that it would be more profitable for him to use his talents to serve their evil needs. Hmmmmmm . . .' He paused as he combed his memory. 'The last I heard of Foggy Glasses – that's what he's known as in crime-fighting circles – he was working on—'

Before Satyr-Man could finish the sentence there was a tremendous explosion which sent the bathroom door sailing through the kitchen wall.

BOOM!!!

Smoke and falling plaster filled the air. Bonita was blown against Satyr-Man and they both landed in a heap in a corner. Books from a bookshelf overhead cascaded down on them.

'You were saying . . . ?' Bonita prompted, dazed, her arms tightly around Satyr-Man's neck.

'He was working on a *waterproof* bomb,' he continued blithely. 'Of course! That's it!' He leaped to his feet. Bonita, still stunned from the bomb burst, looked up at him. 'Foggy Glasses is up to his old tricks. He's trying to eradicate somebody in this room.'

'Who? We don't even know Irving Glasfogel,' Bonita protested as Satyr-Man helped her to her feet.

'Irving who?' Professor Grant groaned. He brushed the plaster off himself and struggled into a sitting position. 'What's all this smoke? What happened?'

'It's nothing serious, Professor,' Satyr-Man said reassuringly.

'Daddy, are you all right?' Bonita asked anxiously.

'I'm in great shape – for a man with no teeth and three broken ribs.' He looked up at the stalwart crime-fighter. 'You still here, son?' Then his eyes travelled to his daughter in her transparent nightie. 'What's been going on here, Bonita? Is this Irving what's-his-name?'

'No, Daddy. This is Satyr-Man. He saved you last night. Remember? And he just saved us all from a fiendish flat-bomb.'

'Ohhhh,' the old man groaned and fell back on the

sofa, clasping his hand to his head. 'Now it's bombs! That damned mummy's curse!'

'Mummies don't plant bombs, Professor,' Satyr-Man explained. 'This is part of an insidious plot. Someone wants to get rid of you . . . or your lovely daughter here.'

'She is lovely, isn't she?' The Professor looked affectionately at Bonita again. 'But I wish she'd forget about all these books and things and find herself a nice man. She's missing a lot in life.'

Bonita blushed prettily, and Satyr-Man tactfully pretended not to notice.

'Think, Professor,' Satyr-Man urged. 'Who would want to do you in?'

'Let me see . . ' The Professor thought the question over. 'There's Dr Thompson . . . He wanted to grab all the credit for the discovery of King Theops' tomb.'

'Dr Thompson, huh? Where does he live?'

'Well . . . he's dead just now. Had a little accident. He was found stabbed in the back with an Arab khanjar. It was the mummy's curse.'

'I guess that let's him off the hook,' Satyr-Man mused. 'Can you think of anybody else?'

'Nope. Can't think of a soul. Can you, Bonita?'

'No, I can't.' She turned to her muscular bed partner. 'Maybe it was all a mistake. Or maybe they were trying to get *you*.'

'I don't think anyone knows I'm here. And I doubt if it was a mistake. Those flat-bombs are very expensive.'

'There . . . there have been some funny things going on at the museum,' the Professor offered hesitantly. 'Ever since I brought that damned mummy back from Egypt.'

'What kind of funny things, Professor?' Satyr-Man asked eagerly.

'Oh . . . windows broken . . . things stolen . . . a guard found impaled on an ancient lance . . .'

'Trivial incidents perhaps,' Satyr-Man noted darkly, 'but they may add up to something sinister . . .'

'Like a mummy's curse?' Bonita chimed in.

'Of course not!' Satyr-Man scoffed. 'Don't tell me you believe in superstitious nonsense like that, Bon – Miss Grant.' As he spoke, the door to the apartment, damaged from the explosion and hanging loose, began to sway, and a mouldy hand wrapped in ancient Egyptian linen reached through the crack. Its bony fingers searched the air and moved toward Satyr-Man's size 17 neck. Bonita Grant alone saw the hand, and her voice stuck in her throat. Her eyes widened with horror and her jaw fell slackly open.

'What's wrong, Miss Grant?' Satyr-Man studied her horrified face with concern. Then, ever alert, he saw the hand reflected in the dark pupils of her staring eyes. With an almost casual movement, he whipped around and grabbed at the hand, catching it in his steely grip. Pulling hard on it, he was astonished to find the hand loosening and coming off in his own fingers. He turned toward Bonita, baffled, holding the disembodied mummy's paw. She squealed and crumpled to the floor in a dead faint. Her thin pyjama top slipped up above her navel, and Satyr-Man paused to admire this sight for a moment before he turned back to the door and threw it open. There was no one in sight in the hallway.

'Aha,' he said to the Professor. 'The mystery is deepening. Someone is definitely trying to frighten you two.'

'And I've got news for you, Satyr-Man,' the Professor said as he cowered on the couch. 'That "someone" is succeeding!'

Satyr-Man smiled inscrutably and bent over Bonita's still form. He picked her up gingerly and placed her gently on a pile of cushions the explosion had scattered. Then he carefully pulled her nightgown down over her hips, shyly averting his eyes.

'I hope she won't be too embarrassed when she realizes . . .' he said gallantly to her father.

'You're a true gentleman, Satyr-Man. The kind any father would be happy to entrust his daughter to,' Professor Grant said warmly. 'But I'm afraid my daughter has no shame. She's a sexologist, you know. Spends all her time spying on mating Eskimos and things like that. I suspect, though, that her own life is rather dull and barren.'

Satyr-Man wisely kept his mouth shut. He examined the mummy's hand and offered it to the Professor.

'What do you make of this, Professor?'

'Hmmmm . . . it does look familiar,' the Professor noted. 'In fact . . . yes . . . I think it's one of the artifacts we found in Egypt. It was stolen from the museum a week ago.'

'I see,' Satyr-Man said gravely. 'Things are beginning to add up. Perhaps I should take a look at this museum of yours.'

'It's closed right now,' the Professor told him sadly. 'You see . . . we've run out of funds. We blew our whole budget on our Egyptian expedition. That's why I came back. I'm trying to raise more money.'

'Perhaps I can help you, Professor. I have a number of wealthy friends.'

'For instance?'

'For instance . . . Parker Potter the Third.'

'Oh, yes . . . I've heard of him.' The Professor frowned. 'Isn't he that notorious playboy and man-about-town?'

'He's the one.'

'A wastrel,' the Professor sneered. 'Anyway, I hear that he hasn't got a dime.'

Satyr-Man winced. Little did the Professor know that the notorious playboy and man-about-town, Parker Potter the Third, was in reality the mysterious nemesis of the underworld – the stalwart and true superhero who was standing before him at this very moment.

'Perhaps not,' Satyr-Man agreed. 'But Parker *does* have a Diners' Club card.'

'Well, since he's a friend of yours . . . I might look

him up, Satyr-Man,' the Professor said politely. Bonita Grant chose this moment to regain consciousness. She moaned softly, making a sound that was very familiar to Satyr-Man. A sound that aroused him erotically. He crossed his legs casually and hoped that Professor Grant wouldn't notice.

'Are you all right, Miss Grant?' he asked solicitously.

'Oh, that awful hand,' she groaned.

Somewhere in the distance a police siren WHEEEED.

'Aha,' Satyr-Man observed keenly, 'some good citizen must have notified the authorities about the explosion here.' He turned to the Professor with a smile. 'And that means that it is time for me to go.' He took the mummy's hand from the Professor, tucked it under his sweat shirt, and headed for the living-room window.

'Will you help us, Satyr-Man?' the Professor asked anxiously.

'You can count on it, Professor Grant. I'll get to the bottom of this mystery. This hand may be a valuable clue.' He bowed toward Bonita. 'And thank you, Miss Grant – for giving me a name, among other things.'

'It was my pleasure, Satyr-Man,' she responded. He raised the window shade and lifted the window. 'But, Satyr-Man . . . there's one more thing . . .'

'I'll be seeing you both again – soon,' Satyr-Man said, not hearing her.

'Wait . . ' she cried, leaping to her feet and heading toward him. But she was too late. With an agile swing, he hurled his feet out the window and catapulted into space. There was a moment of dead silence and then a loud crash sounded in the alley far below.

'I just wanted to tell him that there wasn't any fire escape out there,' she said lamely.

Transmuto, The Metamorphic Myrmidon

by Adrian Cole

Lucian P. Sludge (Lucky to his handful of buddies) struggled with one of the bulging trash cans at the back of *Howie's Burger Bar*. With noisy grunts and puffs he clanged the can up and over the lip of the truck, spilling out the pungent garbage beyond, mindful of any lurking rats (only last week a trashman had been attacked by a pack). Lucky swung the emptied can back and dropped it beside the row, bending cautiously to pick up the next. Cans rattled and banged in the soot-stained alley as the other guys got on with the job, singing and whistling, some cursing the stink of offal. Halfway down the line of overflowing bins, Lucky noticed something – the red bin was out. That was special.

Looking to see if any of the others were watching, Lucky slipped in the back door of *Howie's*, at once assaulted by the billowing aroma of steaming fries and sizzling onion. Holding down his meagre breakfast with difficulty, Lucky went into the phone booth and unhooked the receiver. He dialled a number with his muck-encrusted forefinger. The line buzzed. He put the receiver down and rang again. He did all this five times. The fifth time a voice growled at him from the other end.

'Luigi's Love Parlour.'

'This is his mother.'

'Hold on,' came the voice and Lucky could almost smell garlic fumes – he recognized Ricardo easily enough, one of the Department's heavies.

A moment later, after several clicks, buzzes and unhealthy crackles from the phone, a new voice came on the line. 'Speak,' it commanded.

'Commander? I got your message. Awaiting orders.'

After an impatient cough the voice spoke again. 'That's fine, but hadn't you better identify yourself?'

'Oh yeah . . . it's Trans . . . I mean, Lucky.'

'Ah. Good. Well, this is of vital importance, so I'll come straight to the point. We have a problem. Tell me, Sludge, in your capacity as a trashman, have you noticed anything unusual lately?'

'Well . . . most of the garbage is pretty high, the summer being so hot—'

'No, no! What about vermin? Had much trouble?'

'Yeah – lot more rats about than normal. Feller was chewed up bad last week. Seems like they're getting braver all the time.'

'Right! That's it – rats. We need to get to the root of this problem. City Hall is getting very uptight about it. Lots of night workers have been bitten. Some even gone missing.'

'You mean, this is a job for Transmuto, right?' said Lucky enthusiastically.

'I think it is. You see, these rats are not normal. They seem to be stronger and more virile than normal rats. They breed faster and bigger. And what makes them really lovable is that they seem to have developed a craving for human flesh.'

'I . . . uh, see. Are you sure this is a job that Transmuto can handle?' wheedled Lucky. 'I mean, there must be other guys in the Department better suited. How about Bog Man?'

'Nonsense! No false modesty! We need someone who can slither down into the sewers and meet the enemy on common ground. Transmuto is our man.'

Lucky was too busy swallowing to answer.

'You are to rendezvous with Professor Zealous at coordinate 7 tonight at 10 p.m., got that?'

'Tonight! Gosh, Commander, I don't think I can make that . . . you see, I have to visit my . . . uh, my aged aunt, and I—'

'Remember your Departmental oath! No buts! Cosmopolis is in deadly peril. We must stop this horror from below before it develops into a full scale invasion.'

'*Invasion*? How many of these things are there?'

'That's what we want you to find out. Tonight at 10. Be there.'

Lucky started to prevaricate, but the phone was already dead.

Summer had been a scorcher, but by the evening it had decided to compound Lucky's misery by drizzling. He had never been the most enthusiastic of the Department's super-team. He would have stuck to trash work gladly, even carried out some of the easier, more exciting Transmuto tasks every day, but the tough ones bothered him.

The building blocks of Cosmopolis loomed up into cloud and disappeared. The streets looked gloomy, fire hydrants like tombstones. Lucky slouched along with his hands in his trench coat pockets. Down on the corner of the two wide thoroughfares that constituted coordinate 7, he could see the old newsstand. An aged guy in a thick overcoat waved papers in the air at the occasional bypassers on the street.

Lucky stopped and picked up a paper. 'Okay, professor?' he mumbled.

The other sniffed and busied himself shuffling papers on the stand. 'That's *not* the way to address me,' he hissed through his teeth.

'Sorry.'

'We're supposed to be using code,' growled the Professor irritably. 'You could be anyone.'

'Yeah,' nodded Lucky. 'You're absolutely right. It's too risky taking chances on someone who could be anyone. Maybe we ought to go home, study up the code properly and come back tomorrow. I'll have it right for then, okay?'

'Not so fast,' snapped the Professor, grabbing Lucky by the arm. 'It has to be tonight. I've prepared the serum. Anyway, I recognize you without all that code crap. Did you know you reek, Sludge?'

Lucky muttered something.

'Now, go down that alley. Third manhole. Take the serum and go. It'll last twelve hours. The Commander wants a full report in the morning. See what you can dredge up down there.' The Professor pointed meaningfully to the street beneath his feet.

Lucky took the ampoule of blue serum from the Professor's hand sulkily and made to slip it into a pocket. Keeping a straight face, he made a play of accidentally dropping the ampoule, expecting it to shatter on the tarmac. It bounced.

The Professor glared at him. 'Third manhole.'

Lucky turned and shuffled off. There was nothing else for it. Transmuto would have to get on with the job.

Down the alley, at the third manhole, Lucky stopped. He looked around, but the only pair of eyes that watched him belonged to a curious tom cat that sat on a broken fence. Satisfied, Lucky flipped the tiny cork from the ampoule of serum and gulped the blue liquid down. At once the transformation began. Lucky, clothes, shoes and all, became abruptly transmogrified into a quivering, shapeless mass, an amorphic blob of jelly. The tom cat shrieked as if it had been scorched and shot off into the darkness.

Transmuto slithered towards the heavy manhole lid and began seeping through its holes and cracks. Down the hole beyond his malleable body wriggled, none of it left behind on the street, so that the whole mass plopped down into the drain and settled in the gurgling water that ran by. Quickly he began to activate his metabolic control so that the body reformed itself – he could now chose whatever shape he liked and mould himself into it, also creating whatever colours he wanted, thus simulating if necessary clothes, feathers, scales or other camouflage.

For the time being he decided to become human in form again, although not as the puny Lucky, but as a fairly musclebound specimen. He wasted a bit of time preening himself, then, having flexed his disproportionate muscles and having practised a number of wild, scything karate chops, Transmuto advanced down the running stream of sewage that led farther into the murky darkness. The stench was appalling, and the light almost non-existent. But he had to go forward, as the root of the rat problem would be there somewhere.

Two problems presented themselves. The drain dipped downwards, making it more difficult to walk upon the slippery surface of the pipe, and the light became pitch darkness. The inevitable happened – Transmuto's feet shot from under him and he hit the foul water hard. Just in time, he converted himself into a fish.

That was a mistake. No fish could live in that polluted stuff. Changing back to a man, he came up gagging and coughing, kneeling on all fours and peering through the matted muck of his hair. Human eyes were no help, so he converted them into cat's eyes. Better.

There, not more than twenty yards away, were a dozen or more rats. They were much bigger than normal rats, and a sickly grey pallor, so they had to be the breed he was after. Their red, pin-point eyes blazed at him and he could almost hear their minds ticking over as they debated which of them should rip into his flesh first.

Quickly he reassembled his metabolism. As the rats came on, they now saw before them, not a huge, musclebound, meaty specimen, but a short, emaciated, bony octogenarian, hardly worth a bite. Or so Transmuto thought. But in spite of this inspired defence, the rats came on. Hungrily.

Then another brainwave hit him. He converted into a rat, too, only ten times as big as any of them. He began making appropriate rat noises – aggressive ones. It did the trick. They did an abrupt about turn and darted off down a side drain, tails flicking from side to side like white flags.

Pleased with this result, Transmuto gave chase. Maybe they would lead him to their headquarters. For some time he bounced along the sewer pipe after them, smearing himself in muck and filth, but taking little notice of it. He was a rat. He barely kept the others in view, though it was near impossible to see anything, even with his feline eyes. He was guided largely by their nervous squeaking.

His gleeful pursuit came to an abrupt halt as his body clanged loudly and painfully into something, practically knocking him senseless as he hit it. Thick metal bars had been welded over the entrance to another sewer outlet – the rats had gone through easily, but Transmuto's great bulk had wedged him between the bars. He unscrambled his brains and reduced size.

For a few moments he sat on his haunches in a pool of effluent, dazed. The drain walls seemed to ebb and flow, but he soon recovered his wits. With an experimental twitch of his whiskers, he set off once more in pursuit of the fleeing rats.

He had not gone far, when he saw them creeping stealthily towards him. Giving the rat equivalent of a shout of triumph, he charged. It was not until he was among them, being cuffed and bitten viciously, that he realized he was still only pint-sized for a rat. They had piled on top of him and were giving him a tough time of it before he began to expand himself. The rats flew off one by one as the huge bulk began to fill the entire drain.

Soon the attackers had zipped off down another pipe, baffled by the inconsistency of their enemy. Transmuto let them go, pausing now to weigh his position. Things were moving a shade too fast for his brain. He had to plan ahead. Get things in perspective – literally. He tried to move off, but was stuck fast. Reducing again, he went on. No point just making the rats run. That way they'd never lead him to their top dog, or rather rat.

Cautiously he progressed down the drains, keeping to about the same size as the rats he had seen. No point in arousing suspicion either. After a winding journey down a maze of evil-smelling drains and pipes, sometimes swimming, he came to a fast running torrent of sewage which plunged down into a lake affair. At the far edge of this phosphorescent cauldron of muck was a wide cavern, and gathered on the shore were scores of rats, mostly bloated and bulky, all in apparent conclave, like generals plotting some master campaign. This, mused Transmuto, must be the place he was after.

The squealing and squeaking intensified in volume as the rats ran hither and thither, conferring. How to infiltrate and find out what was afoot? Transmuto watched the flowing sewage. Now and then he made out shapes on its surface – bits of driftwood, old boxes, floating garbage. A good few rats were using these as makeshift craft to get across to the cavern. One of the lumps of rotting wood bumped the drain edge near Transmuto and he quickly scuttled onto it, the stream taking him out over the lake.

For a moment he thought about becoming a spider or a bat or something, but he reckoned the best way to infiltrate would be as a rat. Plenty of them seemed to be gathering – this must be the hinted invasion force. Their discussions seemed disturbingly organized, almost human. Transmuto let the impromptu boat get him to the cavern and hopped ashore. Nonchalantly he ambled (as far as that was possible for a rat) across to the place where the biggest of the rats were holding conference. As he did so, every eye in the place turned to him. None of the rats moved, but they all fell silent.

So much for the discreet infiltration ploy. They were all watching *him*. He looked down at his muck-smeared rat form, half expecting to see six legs, or an extra toe on each foot or something. Presently some of the rats began making odd sounds – not aggressive at all, but sort of . . . encouraging. One or two of them even began to nose up to him. Their expressions had a certain hint of something. Something sexy.

It then dawned on Transmuto why they were all watching him. Correction – her. He had made a hurried changeover and in his haste had become a female rat. All this mob were males. But appreciative males at least. Already they were preparing for a mass demonstration of that appreciation. Transmuto was in a spot – if he quickly transformed himself into a male now, suspicions would be aroused. He could go huge again, but his cover would be blown, or maybe he could just run amok and smash up as many of the rats as he could. But that would be no guarantee of permanent success.

The matter was taken out of his hands before he could figure out another plan. Something whanged down from above. The rats drew back *en masse*. Transmuto was trapped, for a cylindrical glass contraption had dropped over him: he was caught like a specimen in a jam jar. There was only one thing for it – he reduced himself to an amorphous, pulpy jelly, hoping to expand and shatter the walls of the transparent prison.

As he began to change and heave at the walls, a voice came to him from some unseen speaker in the glass. 'It's no use, Transmuto. You're trapped! It isn't glass, it's ultracarb. You'll never crack it, no matter how much pressure you exert.' The disembodied voice ended with a chuckle of confidence. At once Transmuto changed into a mole and began scratching at the floor of his prison. But it was solid rock. What bores through solid rock? he asked himself, but offhand he couldn't think of any creature that could.

He turned himself into a man again and looked around at the rats, whose eyes blazed with virile hate. 'Okay, it looks like I'm stymied. So now what?'

From out of the darkness beyond the rats came a tall figure, face masked in black with only red eye slits showing. The rats drew back from it respectfully as it approached the glass.

'So, you metamorphic moron, you're stuck fast. You can change into as many things as you like, but you won't get out.'

Transmuto sniffed. 'Okay, I'll buy that. But who the heck are you anyway?'

The figure cackled disturbingly. 'I am the Lord of the Vermin.'

Transmuto looked around at the gathered multitude. 'You're . . . the brains behind this horde?'

'That's right, Transmuto. Each and every one of them obeys me. My assistants bred them all in vats. They have been brainwashed to respond to my voice. I have only to command them. See how much bigger than ordinary rats they are? They're prolific breeders, too. And you know what they like to eat most?'

'Yeah – human flesh.'

'That's it.'

'But what's the game? What are you going to do with them all?'

The Lord of the Vermin cackled again, a shade higher up the scale. 'First, I shall let them loose in the very heart of the Cosmopolis. They will chase out everyone and devour anyone foolish enough to stay behind. It will be a lightning attack! Once the centre of the city has been evacuated, I'll have its perimeter patrolled. Then I'll go up there and help myself to as many goodies as I want!'

Transmuto swallowed. 'Yes, of course! Some of the largest diamond corporations in the world are housed in the city centre. You'll be rich—'

'Too right! I'll be *the* richest man in the world. And that's only the start! Once I have the funds, I'll breed more super-rats – super-dogs even, and maybe giant tarantulas and oversize gorillas! There's no limit to what I can do! The world will bow to me!'

'Sounds vaguely familiar,' muttered Transmuto sceptically.

'Yes, others have tried. But with the fabulous wealth I shall have at my disposal, what's to stop me? My assistants are possessed of brilliant minds. There will be ample scope for research.'

'I guess you have a point. No use trying to talk you out of it?'

'Save your breath, Transmuto. You'll need it when I start pumping the air out of that jar!'

Transmuto paled. 'Now, don't get like that. Surely a big shot like you could do with a useful right hand man? I'm pretty versatile, you know.'

'What! You'd break your oath of servitude! You, who are sworn to the protection of Cosmopolis – you'd change sides? I don't believe it!'

Transmuto spread his hands resignedly. 'Why not? You're going to wipe me out.'

The Lord of the Vermin's red eyes narrowed. 'I thought you guys had more spine.'

'Listen, I never wanted in to start with! You know how I got this job? Huh?'

'Of course not—'

'Well, I'll tell you. When I was a kid, I contracted this . . . well, strange kind of biological malfunction . . . like a sort of metabolic mix-up. My mother reckoned it was because I used to play in the rubble of a nuclear waste dumping ground. Anyway, my skin used to do funny things, like glow in the dark and get bloated, or shrunken. The only way the medics could get me straightened out was by giving me shots of this drug, metaplasm. It kept me stable, most of the time. Only thing was, metaplasm was at an early, experimental stage when they shot it to me and it turned out to have a few weird side effects. Like it controlled my condition, but accelerated it, if you see what I mean. I became Transmuto. By now I was addicted to metaplasm anyway. They worked on it and pretty soon had it sophisticated and called it metaplasm-plus. Then the Department got hold of me and said, work for us, or we cut off your rations of metaplasm-plus. So if I don't get a booster of the stuff now and then, I guess I'll reduce down to basics and stay that way. Like jelly.'

The Vermin Lord looked suspicious. 'But if you think you can defect to me, why should it help you? I never said I had any metaplasm-plus.'

'I was coming to that. I know where to get hold of an unlimited supply.'

'Where?'

'If you take over the centre of Cosmopolis, I can get at Professor Zealous' workshop. He's got vats of the stuff.'

The Vermin Lord mused for a bit. 'I don't trust you,' he finally decided.

'But . . . you can't just wipe me out!'

The Lord of the Vermin considered. 'Maybe I won't de-oxygenate, now that you've explained your predicament. I think I'll just leave you in there until you turn into jelly. Then I'll pour you down one of the storm drains. You can have the freedom of the sea! How about that, Transmuto? You can spend the rest of your days as an overweight amoeba!'

Transmuto looked sullen. 'That's not funny.'

'Too bad. But I've got my army. Pretty soon the invasion begins. Tonight, in fact. Right now I've got plans to finalize. So I'll just leave you to it. Enjoy.' Without another word – only another demonic cackle or two – the grim figure stalked off into one of the black drains. Transmuto stared out at the rats, who glared back malignly. Getting out of this would be tough.

He went to the edge of the jar and checked it out, but it seemed to be hermetically sealed. Next he tried studying the ground again, but there were no cracks. It looked like a dead end. The rats were amassed outside, watching his actions curiously. As he looked at them, shuddering, he was glad of the jar after all. They looked ravenous. *Ravenous?* Maybe there was something in that . . .

He tried something: quickly he altered his human form and became a huge, bloated, hideously obese man, with thick jowls wobbling and bulging coils of flab hanging from all parts of him. Arms, legs, neck were all thickened out with bulbous fat. His gut hung over his pants in heavy folds. He had become a quivering mountain of thick, juicy flesh.

The effect on the rats was immediate and one hundred per cent successful. As one they launched themselves at the jar's sides, slavering for the enticing feast, so that in seconds it was covered in squealing, fighting rodents, all madly intent on breaking in to get at the huge mound of living food. Countless thousands of rats joined the assault as Transmuto encouraged them. He could hear the ultracarb groaning under the colossal pressure. It might not crack, but the jar was taking a tremendous pounding.

At last there was a popping sound and Transmuto saw the base of the jar had torn free from the floor of the chamber. In a moment the jar would topple and the striving mass would rush in and chew him up. Hundreds of bodies wriggled under the falling jar, and at once Transmuto became a rat again, so that all was confusion and rats were nipping and biting each other in the mêlée.

Bit by bit, Transmuto, now ignored, started to struggle away from the pressing chaos until he was able to get to the edge of the chamber and take a breather. The rats were so intent on getting at their erstwhile meal that they had lost all reason. Transmuto had to find the Lord of the Vermin before he launched his first major assault on Cosmopolis.

Warily he moved down more complex drain systems, wondering up which of the many pipes the villain could have gone. Suddenly he stopped; he could hear voices indistinctly. The metal pipes carried them. He put his ear to the nearest pipe and the voices came clearer. He figured out the direction. The pipe that seemed to lead off the way he wanted was very narrow, so he broke down into his basic form and began to slither along the pipe, swallowed by darkness. Some way ahead there was a pipe leading upwards and he bubbled up it, coming at length into a much wider pipe. In this there was a grille and beyond a damp, lichen-coated chamber.

In there was the Lord of the Vermin with two other men, both of whom were nodding and bowing subserviently. There were vats and pipes and weird tubes, and as Transmuto turned back into rat form he shuddered – the pipe he had been travelling along originally fed into one of the boiling vats.

'Is he ready?' came the sharp voice of the Vermin Lord.

'Soon,' replied one of the men, who was using a massive ladle to stir the contents of the biggest vat. It contained a repellent mixture and exuded a particularly vile stench.

'The ultimate rat weapon!' cackled the Lord of the Vermin. 'A rat larger than a horse!'

Transmuto blanched at the thought of what must be beneath that seething surface. He had to act fast. The walls of the poorly lit chamber were wet with slime and trickling seepage from above. Transmuto began to alter and then ooze down through the grille to melt into the walls, gathering in a wide pool on the floor of the chamber, behind another of the vats.

'I shall call him Vatilla! My rat army will follow him to the last rat – and he will obey my every command!' cried the Vermin Lord heatedly.

'Indeed he will,' said the white-coated man beside him. 'He has been especially bred to obey only you. You will see.'

Transmuto hadn't got his strategy straightened out, but by chance precipitated a series of events that precluded calculated thought. Having dripped into the chamber fully, he started to change into something more formidable than green slime. A showdown with these three necessitated something ferocious. He tried for a wolf, and as his bulk began to form and proportion itself, he forgot he was partially beneath a vat, so that as he reformed, his shaggy shoulder whacked up under the base of the vat and sent it crashing to the floor. Something brackish and thick plopped out in a viscous tide. The man holding the big ladle yelped as the foul muck lapped at his feet and he gave an involuntary yank on his ladle. The sudden move was enough to rock the big vat. Part of its contents slopped over the side, followed by the whole revolting mass as the vat fell right over. It thumped into the first of a line of smaller vats, all of which clanged over, spilling out more gelatinous matter.

The three men and the startled wolf stared in horror at the writhing revulsion before them. Matter from all the vats had coalesced into one heaving pool of grotesquerie. Basically it was as amorphous as Transmuto himself, but huge rat paws and other smaller rat features protruded from it at random. It was like a huge rodent that had been partially melted down – but added to it were scores of others. Pairs of tiny eyes and mouths winked and snapped from the convulsing monstrosity. The thing was not without motivation, for one of the bigger mouths gaped and made an abrupt snap; the man with the ladle disappeared unpleasantly.

Transmuto doubted the ability of even a mad wolf to subdue the very much alive horror from the vats, and began to ponder on what form to take to destroy it. Already it was reaching out what looked like several hairy pseudopodia in an experimental attempt to engulf him.

At once he became a fly and zipped upwards out of the way for a spell. The thing then turned on its creators and had soon made short work of the white-coated assistant, whose screams and gurgles choked off as he disappeared from sight, enfolded by palpitating coils and teeth.

Only the Lord of the Vermin remained; he had flattened himself up against the back wall of the chamber, mumbling with terror as the thing began to slither forward. He held out a robed arm and mouthed something incoherent. The thing took no notice.

'Vatilla! Get back! Get back I say!'

He had more luck than Canute did, for Vatilla immediately halted, quivering, obeying some subconsciously implanted response, waiting for its next command. Its master gave a high-pitched giggle, realizing that part of the experiment had been a success. Vatilla's collective brains were primed to obey him.

The Lord of the Vermin then began to search the chamber with his blazing eyes. 'Transmuto!' he yelled. 'I know you're in here somewhere! I don't know how you got free of the jar, but this time you may as well give up. See! Vatilla obeys me, just as we planned. My invasion shall go on. With this monster at its head, it can't fail!' He turned to see a spider scuttling across the wall and with a quick smash of his hand, pulped it, studying the remains hopefully.

Transmuto, meanwhile, was trying to figure how to best the monstrous Vatilla. He could easily scram but, if he did, Cosmopolis had had it. Nothing short of a tank could halt that thing.

Or . . . its master. Maybe if he could control it? He watched the Vermin Lord, who was trying to see into all nooks of the chamber, searching him out. How could he kill him and wrest control from him? A quick death, before he could fight back? Then he had it.

Flying overhead, lining himself up directly above the Vermin Lord's head, he altered and became a king cobra, dropping out of the air and coiling round the villain's neck. But clawed hands quickly reached out and dug into his own reptilian neck, and for a moment there was a great struggle as the two fought.

Vatilla bubbled forward, sensing its master's distress, and the Vermin Lord staggered back, holding off that frighful fanged mouth. One of the overturned vats got in the way, and the Vermin Lord hit it and went backwards. The air whooshed out of him as he and the cobra got themselves even more tangled up. Transmuto was given a nasty crack on the head, but as his swimming senses came round, he saw something in front of him that made him laugh, mentally at least. It was the upthrust posterior of the Lord of the Vermin.

Darting forward, he sunk his twin fangs in hard and pumped home as much poison as his transformation allowed, which was a lot of poison. His opponent yelped, shuddering, and Transmuto withdrew, slithering away as fast as he could before Vatilla decided to take a quick revenge. Transmuto was now mulling over several possibilities, hiding in a dark corner, out of the immediate range and vision of his final opponent.

The Lord of the Vermin gave a last spasmodic twitch and went as stiff as cast iron, very dead. Studying him and his odd garb, Transmuto began to change from the cobra into the dead enemy, careful to ensure that he was a dead ringer for him down to the last stitch of clothing. Satisfied, he walked out from his hiding place in full view of the bristling Vatilla.

He held up his hand. 'Withdraw and await orders,' he told it in a perfectly simulated echo of the Vermin Lord's voice as it started to surge forward. A hungry mouth came to within a few feet of him, exuding a revolting breath that rocked the senses. Transmuto tried not to cringe back. But Vatilla stopped inches short and gradually began to pull back.

Relieved, Transmuto told the thing to keep moving, and presently they reached the end of the chamber, which led to a wide drain. The bulk of the rat monster just about squeezed down this, obedient to Transmuto. Following numerous of these wide drains, the two of them came at last to the central cavern, where the multitudes of the rat invasion force were gathered.

Countless eyes fixed themselves on Transmuto. Would the rats be as easily fooled as the brainwashed monster? They seemed to be waiting. Yes, there would be no attack. They wanted orders. For a moment Transmuto drank in the potential power at his fingertips. This huge force . . . and the blubbery Vatilla. He could so easily achieve the same goals as the Lord of the Vermin . . .

But he let the mad notion slip. He just didn't fancy rats as companions for the length of any prospective regnum. He turned to Vatilla and pointed to the rats. 'Attack!' he told it.

The effect was instantaneous. At once the lumbering thing shot out a mass of undulating pseudopodia, and the rat horde knew there was a battle on. It didn't seem to dismay them, for they leapt into the fray with frenzied abandon, and were soon chewing off chunks of monster. Transmuto edged his way round the action, occasionally waving more rats into the fight, making sure that Vatilla didn't see him doing it just in case it was capable of feeling suspicion.

At the end of the cavern, by the lake, Transmuto again became a rat. He paused only to watch the bloody battle as it reached its peak. Great regiments of rats were being engulfed and pulped, while whole sections of Vatilla were being torn to ribbons and shredded. There was a whirlwind of activity and a bedlam of squealing and squeaking. Evidently the rats would rip the thing to bits, but their numbers would be terribly depleted. The invasion force would be so badly mauled that it would lose all efficacy – and without the Lord of the Vermin to command it, it was unlikely that the remnants would venture out to pester Cosmopolis in any great numbers.

Transmuto hopped on a passing piece of jetsam and used his back feet as paddles to get him to the opposite shore. After this he would be only too glad to go back to collecting garbage.

Easy Way Out

by Marion Pitman

A man in a grey flannel suit walked down a New York street. He was going home to supper. His wife had got a job when the children started school, so he was carrying a six-pack of beer and a frozen pizza in a plastic carrier bag. He caught his reflection in a passing window, and decided he needed a haircut.

He turned a corner, and saw up ahead all the traffic was stopped by a mass of people. He sighed. He was late already. Coming closer, he saw half a dozen figures in luridly coloured union suits towering above the rest of the crowd. He swore, and plodded on, muttering 'Damned superheroes. Can't move for 'em. Everywhere you go, city's full of 'em, tearing up the streets, throwing each other around. What're they doing now, holding a convention?'

The crowd seemed to form a circle around something the man in the grey flannel suit couldn't see. On the inside of the circle he recognized Batman, Robin and Superman, all looking baffled; opposite them Iron Man and Captain America were in earnest consultation with Thor, the god of thunder, who was backed by a phalanx of other Norse gods. The onlookers had drawn back from where a large blue figure was seated by itself on the ground, grumbling, 'Bulk doesn't understand.'

The man in the grey flannel suit sighed again. He approached a minor Norse god. 'Excuse me,' he said, 'I'm in rather a hurry; my wife's expecting me—'

The deity shrugged; 'I sympathize with thee. But it is not our doing; thee must take it up with he that doth cause all the trouble, he that doth call himself Supercreep,' and he jerked a thumb towards the centre of the circle.

'I see,' said the man in the grey flannel suit, wishing

they'd teach English grammar in Asgard, 'Thank you,' and he eased his way through towards the thunder god. No-one noticed; he was that kind of man.

Coming out on the inner rim of the circle, he saw its focus. A short, thick man, in a curious costume of orange and purple (the man in the grey flannel suit winced) stood in the road, darting small, close-set eyes from side to side. He looked, even more than the surrounding superheroes, like an advert for someone's body building course, but his stance owed more to the example of the greater apes.

The man in the grey flannel suit stepped into the open space; when he had gone a few yards, the supervillain spotted him.

'Hey!' yelled Supercreep. The man in the grey flannel suit stopped. 'Who're you?' demanded Supercreep.

'My name's Hero,' said the man in the grey flannel suit.

Supercreep laughed; it was not a pleasant sound. '*You're* a hero?' he sneered.

'No, no,' said the man, 'that's my *name*. Joe Hero.'

'And you think you can beat me?' Supercreep was still amused.

Joe Hero sighed; 'I deplore violence, but I guess I'll have to try.'

Supercreep laughed again. The buildings shook, and the Bulk began to growl, deep in his throat. Supercreep stopped laughing.

'D'you know why we're all here?' he shouted. 'We're all waitin' for the mayor of New York to bring me one hundred million dollars. That's my price for not destroyin' the city. An' you know why he's payin' me? Because I am the ultimate villain. I am armoured individually against the superpowers of each and every superhero in New York City.'

' 'tis true,' said Thor. 'Even the mystic powers of we Asgardians cannot prevail against him.'

'Has anyone else tried?' asked Joe Hero. 'I mean, anyone besides gods and superheroes?'

This time everyone laughed except Joe Hero, and the Blue Bulk, who was still trying to figure it all out. The buildings shook for several blocks.

When the laughter died, Supercreep said, 'Look, Hero, I've already killed thirty two people this afternoon; you wanna make it thirty three?'

'Am I to take that as a threat?' inquired Joe Hero.

'Yeah, that's a threat.' The archvillain was beginning to get angry. 'You're a punk, that's what you are, nothing but a goddam punk.'

'Oh, I hope not,' murmured Joe Hero. 'I suppose I shall have to try.' He put down his plastic carrier, took out a small-calibre hand-gun, and shot Supercreep through the left eye.

When Supercreep hit the street, the whole of New York shook. When the vibrations had stopped, there was a stillness. Somewhere a woman had hysterics, but all the superheroes were very quiet, staring at Supercreep, who looked very dead.

Joe Hero picked up his plastic bag and went home. He heard a low murmur – 'Bulk still doesn't understand.'

It's a Bird, It's a Plane!

by Norman Spinrad

Dr Felix Funck fumblingly fitted yet another spool onto the tape recorder hidden in the middle drawer of his desk as the luscious Miss Jones ushered in yet another one. Dr Funck stared wistfully for a long moment at Miss Jones, whose white nurse's smock advertised the contents most effectively without revealing any of the more intimate and interesting details. If only x-ray vision were really possible and not part of the infernal Syndrome . . .

Get a hold of yourself, Funck, get a hold of yourself! Felix Funck told himself for the seventeenth time that day.

He sighed, resigned himself, and said to the earnest-looking young man whom Miss Jones had brought to his office, 'Please sit down, Mr . . .?'

'Kent, Doctor,' said the young man, seating himself primly on the edge of the overstuffed chair in front of Funck's desk. 'Clark Kent!'

Dr Funck grimaced, then smiled wanly, 'Why not?' he said, studying the young man's appearance. The young man wore an archaic blue double-breasted suit and steel-rimmed glasses. His hair was steel-blue.

'Tell me . . . Mr Kent,' he said, 'do you by some chance know where you are?'

'Certainly, Doctor,' replied Clark Kent crisply. 'I'm in a large public mental hospital in New York City!'

'Very good, Mr Kent. And do you know why you're here?'

'I think so, Dr Funck!' said Clark Kent. 'I'm suffering from partial amnesia! I don't remember how or when I came to New York!'

'You mean you don't remember your past life?' asked Dr Felix Funck.

'Not at all, Doctor!' said Clark Kent. 'I remember everything up till three days ago when I found myself suddenly in New York! And I remember the last three days here! But I don't remember how I got here!'

'Well then, where did you live before you found yourself in New York, Mr Kent?'

'Metropolis!' said Clark Kent. 'I remember that very well! I'm a reporter for the Metropolis *Daily Planet*! That is, I am if Mr White hasn't fired me for not showing up for three days! You must help me, Dr Funck! I must return to Metropolis immediately!'

'Well then you should just hop the next plane for home,' suggested Dr Funck.

'There don't seem to be any flights from New York to Metropolis!' exclaimed Clark Kent. 'No buses or trains either! I couldn't even find a copy of the *Daily Planet* at the Times Square newsstand! I can't even remember where Metropolis is! It's as if some evil force has removed all traces of Metropolis from the face of the Earth! That's my problem, Dr Funck! I've got to get back to Metropolis, but I don't know how!'

'Tell me, Mr Kent,' said Funck slowly, 'just why is it so imperative that you return to Metropolis immediately?'

'Well . . . uh . . . there's my job!' Clark Kent said uneasily. 'Perry White must be furious by now! And there's my girl, Lois Lane! Well, maybe she's not my girl yet, but I'm hoping!'

Dr Felix Funck grinned conspiratorially. 'Isn't there some more pressing reason, Mr Kent?' he said. 'Something perhaps having to do with your Secret Identity?'

'S-secret Identity?' stammered Clark Kent. 'I don't know what you're talking about, Dr Funck!'

'Aw come on, Clark!' Felix Funck said. 'Lots of people have Secret Identities. I've got one myself. Tell me yours, and I'll tell you mine. You can trust me, Clark. Hippocratic Oath, and like that. Your secret is safe with me.'

'*Secret?* What secret are you talking about?'

‘Come, come, Mr Kent!’ Funck snapped. ‘If you want help, you’ll have to come clean with me. Don’t give me any of that meek, mild-mannered reporter jazz. I know who you really are, Mr Kent.’

‘I’m Clark Kent, meek, mild-mannered reporter for the Metropolis *Daily Planet*!’ insisted Clark Kent.

Dr Felix Funck reached into a desk drawer and produced a small chunk of rock coated with green paint. ‘Who is in reality, Superman,’ he exclaimed, ‘faster than a speeding bullet, more powerful than a locomotive, able to leap tall buildings at a single bound! Do you know what this is?’ he shrieked, thrusting the green rock in the face of the hapless Clark Kent. ‘It’s Kryptonite, that’s what it is, genuine government-inspected Kryptonite! How’s *that* grab you, Superman?’

Clark Kent, who is in reality the Man of Steel, tried to say something, but before he could utter a sound, he lapsed into unconsciousness.

Dr Felix Funck reached across his desk and unbuttoned Clark Kent’s shirt. Sure enough, underneath his street clothing, Kent was wearing a pair of moth-eaten longjohns dyed blue, on the chest of which a rude cloth ‘S’ had been crudely sewn.

‘Classic case . . .’ Dr Funck muttered to himself. ‘Right out of a textbook. Even lost his imaginary powers when I showed him the phoney Kryptonite. Another job for Supershrink!’

Get a hold of yourself, Funck, get a hold of yourself! Dr Funck told himself again.

Shaking his head, he rang for the orderlies.

After the orderlies had removed Clark Kent No. 758, Dr Felix Funck pulled a stack of comic books out of a desk drawer, spread them out across the desktop, stared woodenly at them and moaned.

The Superman Syndrome was getting totally out of hand. In this one hospital alone, there are already 758 classified cases of Superman Syndrome, he thought forlornly, and lord knows how many Supernuts in the receiving ward awaiting classification.

'Why? Why? Why?' Funck muttered, tearing at his rapidly thinning hair.

The basic, fundamental, inescapable, incurable reason, he knew was, of course, that the world was full of Clark Kents. Meek, mild-mannered men. Born losers. None of them, of course, had self-images of themselves as nebbishes. Every mouse has to think of himself as a lion. Everyone has a Secret Identity, a dream image of himself, possessed of fantastic powers, able to cope with normally impossible situations . . .

Even psychiatrists had Secret Identities, Funck thought abstractedly. After all, who but Supershrink himself could cope with a ward full of Supermen?

Supershrink! More powerful than a raving psychotic! Able to diagnose whole neuroses in a single session! Faster than Freud! Abler than Adler! Who, disguised as Dr Felix Funck, balding, harried head of the Superman Syndrome ward of a great metropolitan booby-hatch, fights a never-ending war for Adjustment, Neo-Freudian Analysis, Fee-splitting, and the American Way!

Get a hold of yourself, Funck, get a hold of yourself!

There's a little Clark Kent in the best of us, Funck thought.

That's why Superman had long since passed into folklore. Superman and his alter ego Clark Kent were the perfect, bald statement of the human dilemma (Kent) and the corresponding wish-fulfilment (The Man of Steel). It was normal for kids to assimilate the synthetic myth into their grubby little ids. But it was also normal for them to outgrow it. A few childhood schizoid tendencies never hurt anyone. All kids are a little loco, Funck reasoned sagely.

If only someone had shot Andy Warhol before it was too late!

That's what opened the whole fetid can of worms,

Funck thought – the Pop Art craze. Suddenly, comic books were no longer greasy kid stuff. Suddenly, comic books were Art with a big, fat capital 'A'. They were hip, they were in, so-called adults were no longer ashamed to snatch them away from the brats and read the things themselves.

All over America, meek, mild-mannered men went back and relived their youths through comic books. Thousands of meek, mild-mannered slobs were once more coming to identify with the meek, mild-mannered reporter of the Metropolis *Daily Planet*. It was like going home again. Superman was the perfect wish-fulfilment figure. No one doubted that he could pulverize 007, leap over a traffic jam on the Long Island Expressway in a single bound, see through women's clothing with his x-ray vision, and *voilà*, the Superman Syndrome!

Step one: the meek, mild-mannered victim identified with that prototype of all *schlemiels*, Clark Kent.

Step two: they began to see themselves more and more as Clark Kent; began to dream of themselves as Superman.

Step three: a moment of intense frustration, a rebuff from some Lois Lane figure, a dressing-down from some irate Perry White surrogate, and something snapped, and they were in the clutches of the Superman Syndromc.

Usually, it started covertly. The victim procured a pair of longjohns, dyed them blue, sewed an 'S' on them, and took to wearing the costume under his street clothes occasionally, in times of stress.

But once the first fatal step was taken, the Superman Syndrome was irreversible. The victim took to wearing the costume all the time. Sooner or later, the stress and strain of reality became too much, and a fugue-state resulted. During the fugue, the victim dyed his hair Superman steel-blue, bought a blue double-breasted suit and steel-rimmed glasses, forgot who he was, and woke up one morning with a set of memories straight out of the comic book. He *was* Clark Kent, and he had to get back to Metropolis.

Bad enough for thousands of nuts to waltz around thinking they were Clark Kent. The horrible part was that Clark Kent was the Man of Steel. Which meant that thousands of grown men were jumping off buildings, trying to stop locomotives with their bare hands, tackling armed criminals in the streets and otherwise contriving to commit *hara-kiri*.

What was worse, there were so many Supernuts popping up all over the place that everyone in the country had seen Superman at least once by now, and enough of them had managed to pull off some feat of daring – saving a little old lady from a gang of muggers, foiling an inexpert bank robbery simply by getting underfoot – that it was fast becoming impossible to convince people that there *wasn't* a Superman.

And the more people became convinced that there was a Superman, the more people fell victim to the Syndrome, the more people became convinced . . .

Funck groaned aloud. There was even a well-known television commentator who jokingly suggested that maybe Superman *was* real, and the nuts were the people who thought he wasn't.

Could it be? Funck wondered. If sanity was defined as the norm, the mental state of the majority of the population, and the majority of the population believed in Superman, then maybe anyone who didn't believe in Superman had a screw loose . . .

If the nuts were sane, and the sane people were nuts, and the nuts were the majority, then the truth would have to be . . .

'Get a hold of yourself, Funck!' Dr Felix Funck shouted aloud. 'There is no Superman! There is no Superman!'

Funck scooped the comics back into the drawer and pressed a button on his intercom.

'You may send in the next Supertwitch, Miss Jones,' he said.

Luscious Miss Jones seemed to be blushing as she ushered the next patient into Dr Funck's office.

There was something unsettling about this one, Funck decided instantly. He had the usual glasses and the usual blue double-breasted suit, but on him they looked almost good. He was built like a brick outhouse, and the steel-blue dye job on his hair looked most professional. Funck smelled money. One of the powers of Supershrink, after all was the uncanny ability to instantly calculate a potential patient's bank balance. Maybe there would be some way to grab this one for a private patient . . .

'Have a seat, Mr Kent,' Dr Funck said. 'You are Clark Kent, aren't you?'

Clark Kent sat down on the edge of the chair, his broad back ramrod-straight. 'Why, yes, Doctor!' he said. 'How did you know?'

'I've seen your stuff in the Metropolis *Daily Planet*, Mr Kent,' Funck said. Got to really humour this one, he thought. There's money here. That dye job's so good it must've set him back fifty bucks! *Indeed* a job for Supershrink! 'Well just what seems to be the trouble, Mr Kent?' he said.

'It's my memory, Doctor!' said Clark Kent. 'I seem to be suffering from a strange form of amnesia!'

'So-o . . .' said Felix Funck soothingly. 'Could it possibly be that . . . that you suddenly found yourself in New York without knowing how you got here, Mr Kent?' he said.

'Why that's amazing!' exclaimed Clark Kent. 'You're one hundred percent correct!'

'And could it also be,' suggested Felix Funck, 'that you feel you must return to Metropolis immediately? That, however, you can find no plane or train or bus that goes there? That you cannot find a copy of the *Daily Planet* at the out-of-town newsstands? That, in fact, you cannot even remember where Metropolis is?'

Clark Kent's eyes bugged. 'Fantastic!' he exclaimed. 'How could you know all that? Can it be that you are no ordinary psychiatrist, Dr Funck? Can it be that Dr Felix Funck, balding, harried head of a ward in a great metropolitan booby-hatch is in reality . . . *Supershrink?*'

'Ak!' said Dr Felix Funck.

'Don't worry, Dr Funck,' Clark Kent said in a warm, comradely tone, 'your secret is safe with me! We superheroes have got to stick together, right?'

'Guk!' said Dr Felix Funck. How could he possibly know? he thought. Why, he'd have to be . . . *ulp!* That was ridiculous. Get a hold of yourself, Funck, get a hold of yourself! Who's the psychiatrist here, anyway?

'So you know that Felix Funck is Supershrink, eh?' he said shrewdly. 'Then you must also know that you can conceal nothing from me. That I know your Secret Identity too.'

'*Secret Identity?*' said Clark Kent piously. 'Who me? Why everyone knows that I'm just a meek, mild-mannered reporter for a great metropolitan—'

With a savage whoop, Dr Felix Funck suddenly leapt halfway across his desk and ripped open the shirt of the dumbfounded Clark Kent, revealing a skin-tight blue uniform with a red 'S' insignia emblazoned on the chest. Top-notch job of tailoring too, Funck thought approvingly.

'Aha!' exclaimed Funck. 'So Clark Kent, meek, mild-mannered reporter, is, in reality, *Superman!*'

'So my secret is out!' Clark Kent said stoically. 'I sure hope you believe in Truth, Justice and the American way!'

'Don't worry, Clark old man. Your secret is safe with me. We superheroes have got to stick together, right?'

'Absolutely!' said Clark Kent. 'Now about my problem, Doctor . . .'

'Problem?'

'How am I going to get back to Metropolis?' asked

Clark Kent. 'By now, the forces of evil must be having a field day!'

'Look,' said Dr Funck. 'First of all, there is no Metropolis, no *Daily Planet*, no Lois Lane, no Perry White, and *no Superman*. It's all a comic book, friend.'

Clark Kent stared at Dr Funck worriedly. 'Are you feeling all right, Doctor?' he asked solicitously. 'Sure you haven't been working too hard? Everybody knows there's a Superman! Tell me, Dr Funck, when did you first notice this strange malady? Could it be that some childhood trauma has caused you to deny my existence? Maybe your mother—'

'Leave my mother out of this!' shrieked Felix Funck. 'Who's the psychiatrist here, anyway? I don't want to hear any dirty stories about my mother. There is no Superman, you're not him, I can prove it!'

Clark Kent nodded his head benignly. 'Sure you can, Dr Funck!' he soothed.

'Look! Look! If you were Superman you wouldn't have any problem. You'd—' Funck glanced nervously about his office. It was on the tenth floor. It had one window. The window had steel bars an inch and a quarter thick. He can't hurt himself, Funck thought. Why not? Make him face reality, and break the delusion!

'You were saying, Doctor?' said Clark Kent.

'If you were Superman, you wouldn't have to worry about trains or planes or buses. You can fly, eh? You can bend steel in your bare hands? Well then why don't you just rip the bars off the window and fly back to Metropolis?'

'Why . . . why you're absolutely right!' exclaimed Clark Kent. 'Of course!'

'Ah . . .' said Funck. 'So you see you have been the victim of a delusion. Progress, progress. But don't think you've been completely cured yet. Even Supershrink isn't *that* good. This will require many hours of private consultation, at the modest hourly rate of a mere fifty dollars. We must uncover the basic psychosomatic causes for the—'

'What are you talking about?' exclaimed Clark Kent, leaping up from the chair and shucking his suit with blinding speed, revealing a full-scale Superman costume, replete with expensive-looking scarlet cape which Funck eyed greedily.

He bounded to the window. 'Of course!' said Superman. 'I can bend steel in my bare hands!' So saying, he bent the inch-and-a-quarter steel bar in his bare hands like so many lengths of liquorice whip, ripped them aside and leapt to the windowsill.

'Thanks for everything, Dr Funck!' he said. 'Up! Up! And away!' He flung out his arms and leapt from the tenth-floor window.

Horrified, Funck bounded to the window and peered out, expecting to see an awful mess on the crowded sidewalk below. Instead:

A rapidly-dwindling caped figure soared out over the New York skyline. From the crowded streets below, shrill cries drifted up to the ears of Dr Felix Funck.

'Look! Up there in the sky!'

'It's a bird!'

'It's a plane!'

'It's SUPERMAN!!'

Dr Felix Funck watched the Man of Steel execute a smart left bank and turn due west at the Empire State Building. For a short moment, Dr Funck was stunned, nonplussed. Then he realized what had happened and what he had to do.

'He's nuts!' Felix Funck shouted. 'The man is crazy! He's got a screw loose. He thinks he's Superman, and he's so crazy that he *is* Superman! The man needs help; *This* is a job for SUPERSHRINK!'

So saying, Dr Felix Funck bounded to the windowsill, doffed his street clothes, revealing a gleaming skin-tight red suit with a large blue 'S' emblazoned across it, and leapt out the window screaming 'Wait for me, Superman, you pathetic neurotic, you, wait for me!'

Dr Felix Funck, who is, after all, in reality Supershrink, turned due west and headed out across the Hudson for Metropolis, somewhere beyond Secaucus, New Jersey.

Up, Up and Away

by Allan C. Kimball

He sat in the large leather easy chair staring out of his window. He sat loosely and listlessly even though he was the most powerful man in the world.

Couldn't he leap tall buildings in a single bound? Wasn't he faster than a speeding locomotive? All outdated analogies, to be sure, but accurate still. But the tall muscular figure sat depressed, his chin supported by a hand that could slay a thousand men in one blow.

Everyone had thought he was some kind of a nut the first time they saw him all dressed up in his suit of black leather with blue piping and the eagle feathers tied with rawhide. Everyone knew 'Supermen' were just in comic books so when he said he was the Avenger, come to right wrongs and fight crime and save lives, well, everyone laughed. They stopped laughing when he helped a demolition company destroy a hotel. With one well-placed blow from his fist. Down the hotel tumbled in dust and timbers and the crowd stood awed and the newspapermen forgot to take the pictures and although the television cameras recorded the event for posterity all the commentators were silent until they caught their breaths and minds and regained their composure. They had stopped laughing when his x-ray vision trapped burglars on the scene and his great strength helped prevent train disasters and plane crashes and his great speed prevented numerous auto accidents. All because of that meteor that had crashed in his backyard on the farm and bathed him in some form of radiation he had yet to figure out. The only thing in the world now that could hurt him was lead, which presented a large enough problem since that material was so common.

He thanked his lucky stars for the prevalence of plastics.

The loneliness of being the most powerful man in the world had been weighing in against him for many years. It was coming to a disastrous head. He longed for the peace and quiet he now no longer could have. He wished for anonymity. He had tried to regain some privacy by adopting the time-honoured secret identity. He became an insurance salesman; disguised by glasses and a fake moustache, he became Herman Glimpshire.

He sat in Herman Glimpshire's apartment, in Herman Glimpshire's clothes, looking very much like Herman Glimpshire. He tore the glasses and moustache off his face in a smooth motion and threw them across the room. He stood up and ripped the leisure suit off his back. 'Damn Herman Glimpshire!' he yelled. But not too loud. Out of habit, he pulled his scream, just as he pulled his punches when fighting criminals, just as he pulled his embraces with Sally Rogers.

Sally Rogers, who was in love with The Avenger, but hated Herman Glimpshire. The same man. All she loved was the power and the glory and the image of The Avenger. His real personality, that he let surface in Herman Glimpshire, left her cold. She would love him if he were green and had one large eye in his forehead . . . like the Xcroxians he fought last week. He was forever saving the world. And for what? He could see the corruption all around him, the corruption that festered and grew. The crime that increased every month in spite of all his efforts. His super-human efforts. Why was he doing all this? He saved the world an average of four times each month according to his latest calculations. What did he get for it? The world generally never even knew about it. But what did they care? Houston had a Superman week each year where he had to put up with spoiled kids and give each of them a ride through the air. There now was an Avenger, Illinois and an Avenger, Arkansas. The Avenger comic books, colouring books, TV shows, cartoons, and suits flourished. He'd begun a whole new wave of fashion. He got nothing while others got rich. He got no percentage of the profits. Even Sally Rogers was getting rich and famous through simple association with The Avenger. She sold all her stories to the newspapers and TV. She'd been interviewed by at least a hundred magazines on her relationship with this super-hero and she had a bestseller on the stands. But she could not love him as himself. Only the muscular black-and-blue-suited hero. He sometimes hated Sally Rogers very much. He had at one time repeatedly teased her about a strawberry birthmark on the inside of her left thigh. He could see everything with that good old x-ray vision. It embarrassed her for a while but then she took it as a sign of intimacy and bothered him even more. Sometimes he thought he should make love to her and teach her a lesson. But he could never make love to a normal person again. In the heat of his passions he might get carried away and his lover could become the innocent victim of his emotions. A simple embrace could crush a Sherman tank. An ejaculation would be like a high-speed bullet.

He looked at himself in the mirror. Tall and stalwart, a symbol of freedom and justice. He scowled. He remembered with deep bitterness the court case last month that had freed a gangster kingpin. Using his super-vision and super-hearing he had discovered a plot to rob Fort Knox. He brought the mobsters in. The federal court judge had thrown the case out, however, on the grounds that the criminals' constitutional right of privacy had been violated by The Avenger. He now had a court injunction sitting on his desk forbidding him to use either power until the case could be finally decided. The gangsters had even sued him for invasion of privacy and defamation of character and use of undue force and prior restraint and a host of other charges that netted them a cool $4,000,000. The uproar the case had caused was still going on. Congress at that very moment was debating the legality of The Avenger's use of his various super-powers. Didn't x-ray vision and super-hearing constitute invasion of privacy. Wasn't The Avenger prejudiced after crime fighting for so many years?

A supersonic buzz filled his super-ears and he sat back down in his chair. It was Sally Rogers again. Why he ever gave her that signal device he'd never know. Day and night she pressed the button and The Avenger, like a faithful dog, came running. Half the time Sally got into ridiculous situations through sheer stupidity. The other half she was just showing off to friends and members of the Avenger Fan Club. He remembered the time when he had returned from the distant planet of Mbi and was taking a hot shower. The signal sounded and he rushed to Sally's aid. When he arrived he had to autograph 200 photographs for local peace officers.

Sally's sonic signal sounded again and interrupted his thoughts. He looked out the window. On top of the Shell Building, Sally was being molested by three thugs. He concentrated and turned his telescopic vision on. He saw that the men struggling with Sally were the same gangsters who had plotted the robbery of Fort Knox. He wished them luck. Sally screamed for help. The noise grated against his super-inner-ear.

'I'm not your personal Avenger!' he yelled. It was unrestrained. The yell startled the gangsters and Sally. The yell startled the world.

The super-voice was heard on the streets of London, Moscow, Melbourne, Hong Kong, Calcutta, Keflavik, Montreal, Los Angeles and Luchenbach. People stopped whatever they were doing all over the world and looked.

He ripped the super-costume off and flung it out the window. He stood naked, watching the world. He laughed to himself. He turned and walked into his bedroom, where he opened a secret door in his closet. The Avenger removed a small gold box and opened it slowly. A deadly grey glow shimmered from the metal inside the box. The grey metal was a bullet. Painfully, The Avenger picked up the lead bullet and placed it in an old souvenir ·38 revolver. With a smile of spite he put the revolver to his temple and pulled the trigger.

Alternative Ending

by Frank Adey

There was a massive, grating rumble at the lower level of audibility, and the wide marble floor of the apartment gave a shuddering sideways lurch. The scientist instinctively flung out an arm, bracing himself against an instrument panel.

The east wall of the chamber was transparent, and looked out over the spires and suspended roadways of the city. Tiny sparklets of light were spilling down from the heights of the nearby towers towards the teeming concourse half a mile below.

'Windows. The tremor shook them loose,' explained the scientist, more to himself than to his frightened wife. 'The vibrations are magnified towards the tops of the buildings. The uppermost floors must be swinging dozens of feet out of place.'

He had a sudden mental vision of what it must be like inside one of the great towers. Hundreds of floors, and on each a terrified mob battering at jammed elevator doors. He thrust the image away, forcing himself to concentrate on his instruments.

'That last shock—' began the woman.

'Was only the beginning. The next quake should hit in ten minutes' time, and the next five minutes after that. The force of the tremors will increase mathematically. Within an hour the internal stresses will become too powerful for the crust to contain.'

'And the planet will explode,' finished his wife quietly. She wondered how he managed to maintain such calm. Perhaps he had been preparing for today for so long that the reality of the catastrophe no longer held any urgency for him. He was studying his display units quite dispassionately, as though someone else's world, other than his own, was about to die.

He turned to her abruptly, and for the first time she saw fear in his eyes.

'Get the boy,' he said.

'Must we?' She felt a terrible helplessness.

'We have no time for further discussions. We both agreed – it will be his only chance.'

She turned in desperate appeal to the unfeeling instruments.

'But supposing you're *wrong*! What if your calculations—'

She stopped short, her hope finally killed by the cold resolve in his eyes. There was no mistake; they had both lived with the truth for too many months to reject it now. Yet only now had the horror become truly real to her, finally assuming a personal shape.

Her husband took her hands. 'Please get the baby,' he said softly.

A fierce, unreasoning possessiveness took hold of her.

'What is the *point*?' she hissed. 'Why send him to die on some empty world at the end of the galaxy? Here, at least we shall all die together! You're condemning your son to die alone! You—'

He slapped her face. The marble walls threw back the sound deafeningly. She fell suddenly into his arms, her body shaking silently.

'He will not be alone,' he said at length. 'There are intelligent, humanoid creatures there. We have both heard their radio messages. And – because conditions there are much milder than the ones we've evolved under – he'll be the strongest, healthiest creature in their world. If he reaches the Earth, his survival is assured. Please give him the chance.' He gently turned her tear-stained face up to his. 'It's the last favour I'll ever ask of you.'

The child was fretful, for the earthquake had jarred him from his afternoon sleep. He struggled feebly in his mother's arms, his tiny face red with anger. She kissed and rocked him, but his crying only grew louder.

Through a blur of tears, she saw her husband haul back the sliding doors to the small observatory.

The small spacecraft – first and last of its kind that its world would ever produce – was poised on a ramp that led up to and through the great opening in the domed roof. The aperture framed a few wisps of cirrus cloud, which the giant red sun of the planet, sinking low in the lateness of the afternoon, had turned to strands of beaten copper. It was a beautiful day for the world to end on.

The baby's crying became more spasmodic as they strapped him carefully into the tiny craft's interior. He blinked damply, curious as his father attached the wires and catheters of his life-support system.

'He should be in hyperspace for about three days. I think I've taken care of all the physical problems; and I'm hoping to allay sensory deprivation symptoms by means of a coloured light display and periodic recordings of household sounds—'

He was speaking quickly, breathlessly now.

The baby smiled up at him from the plastic web of the ship's artificial womb. The scientist tried to smile back, but his vision misted. Dimly he saw the child extend an exploratory hand toward him; the pudgy fist opened like a small pink flower. The scientist shut his eyes firmly, and closed the hatch cover.

And then his wife was upon him like a wildcat, punching and scratching. As he reeled back, one eye burning from the slash of a sharp nail, she flung herself upon the spacecraft, her fingers scrabbling vainly on the dull cylinder. There was the audible cracking of a fingernail, and a little beadlet of blood scurried like mercury over the resistant metal.

Then it was over, the well of her emotions completely drained. She subsided limply over the closed hatch, sobbing thickly. At length she pushed her hair aside, and pressed her ear to the metal.

'At least he isn't crying,' she said brokenly.

It was pointless to tell her that the hull was soundproof.

By the time the final quake began the capsule was nearly two million miles out into space. The city from which it had been launched had already ceased to exist, its towers overwhelmed by the fury of an ocean torn from its bed. As the planet entered its final agony, the child lay asleep, chuckling at a pleasant dream.

The world burst apart at the equator, where the internal stresses were at their greatest. Vast arms of incandescent magma pinwheeled out from the ruined world, creating a miniature galaxy whose centre, although virtually hidden by thousand-mile deep clouds of rubble, still radiated a blue-white nuclear glare.

Even if the child had had at its disposal the means to observe this spectacle, it could have done so only for a second. As the ship's sensors picked up the surge of radiation, it transferred instantaneously into the rippling, jewelled darkness of hyperspace.

It landed in the American Midwest.

The farm was old, an archipelago of dark wooden buildings in a tawny ocean of sun-dried grassland. A mile-long dust track separated it from the outside world. The skeletal black sails of a windmill turned slowly above a sluggish artesian well, emitting an irregular, protesting clatter. The farmer's wife was used to its noise; it was the only sound she expected to hear on that warm, July afternoon.

She paused, one bony hand closing around a fistful of corn as the chickens fussed and gobbled about her feet.

'Hush up, you foolish birds,' she said. She shaded her eyes, pushing back a wandering lock of silver hair. The sunlight winked on her old-fashioned spectacles as she peered up at the sky.

There was a high, hollow, rushing sound. Something fast and far away, coming nearer. The noise climbed steadily to a high-velocity scream. The woman backed into the protective shadow of the barn, anxiously searching the innocent white turrets of summercloud. Then—

'Land *sakes*!'

It came in low, almost brushing the windmill, whose sails whirled in an arthritic frenzy. For a second the metal of it flashed in the sun like a polished kettle; then it was gone, hurtling from view behind the grain silo. Almost at once the concussion of its impact jarred the ground beneath the woman's feet.

She stood, frightened and bewildered, waiting for the windmill-sails to resume their familiar rhythm. Her husband knew something about aircraft, but he was in town.

'It must have landed in the north meadow,' she told the chickens.

After a while, when she had convinced herself that it would not explode, and that there was little fear of having to view the mutilated body of a dead aeronaut, she nerved herself to approach it.

The ground north of the farm rose up sharply towards a nearby ridge. It had therefore intercepted the downward trajectory of the spaceship at a steep angle. The craft had ploughed a deep trench for itself; only one shining fin showed above a wall of tumbled earth. Round about, the grass had flared to a gritty black stubble; now the brief fire was out, and thin blue smoke flowed lazily across the meadow.

Treading gingerly over the broken sods, the farmer's wife peered down into the smoking ditch. Even as she began mentally to delineate the torpedo shape under the fallen earth, the hatch popped open.

Her heart leaped against her ribs. It was a bomb, after all, and with a trick detonator! The strange, escaping scents of an alien world slipped by her unheeded.

Then there was a movement amongst the tangle of

wires and cables within the hatch, and the baby began to cry.

For the first and only time in her life, the farmer's wife took the name of the Lord in vain.

'Well,' said the doctor, packing his shapeless leather bag, 'I got to admit I'm at a loss. That is the most remarkable infant I have ever seen.'

He smiled reassuringly at the middle-aged couple who watched him anxiously across the kitchen table. The farmer, a strong, kindly-looking man in dungarees, kept an arm protectively around his wife's shoulders.

'What about it, Doc? Is he going to be all right?'

The bag closed with a sharp snap.

'Listen,' said the doctor, 'that child was fired into the hillside, at the-Lord-knows-how many miles per hour, in a glorified artillery shell. By rights, he shouldn't have an unbroken bone in his body. Yet not only is he perfectly okay, but he's the healthiest child I've seen in this county all year. Damn sight too healthy, if you ask me.'

'What do you mean?' asked the farmer's wife with some asperity.

The doctor rolled up his shirtsleeve. On the inside of his arm was a small, rapidly blackening bruise.

'Looks like you got hit by a hammer,' said the farmer.

'Nope – baby just did it. Caught me a backhander as I was examining him. He didn't seem to feel a thing – just kept on chuckling. And another thing. I've been trying to get his bloodgroup. Turns out to be impossible. I've broken three needles on his skin. Oh, I'll drop by with a couple more this evening, just in case, but I reckon the result'll be the same. Might as well try sticking them in an anvil.'

'But how can that be?'

'I don't know. Maybe if we knew where he came from we'd have a few answers.'

'You think maybe he's from a foreign country?'

'Maybe further'n that,' said the doctor thoughtfully.

'Did you notice the metal that rocket thing was made of? Not a scratch, not a mark. I reckon it's as indestructible as he is. I don't know of any country on earth that could forge an alloy like that. Anyway, I'll have to report all this to the police. Let them worry about it.' He turned to leave.

The farmer and his wife exchanged a swift, nervous glance. The farmer cleared his throat and stepped forward.

'Say, Doc,' he said, 'until you turn up some folks for him, will it be okay if he stays here? It's – ah – kind of good company having him around.' He glanced back at his wife, who blushed and stared at the ground. 'Maybe if no-one comes along to claim him—'

'Now, hold on,' said the doctor softly. 'Sure, you can look after him for now – can't imagine him being in better hands – but don't go getting too attached to him. I'd hate to see nice folks like yourselves getting themselves hurt.'

He turned in the doorway on his way out, rubbing his arm ruefully. 'And watch out for that uppercut of his!'

It was much later. The farmer and his wife sat at the kitchen table, quietly watching the baby. He lay in a makeshift crib – an old crate padded out with thick blankets. A neighbour had lent a feeding bottle, and a bead of milk still clung to a corner of the child's mouth. He was asleep. The woman stroked the back of a small hand with her finger.

'Imagine,' she said, 'him being so strong and healthy. And with skin like steel! You're going to be a very important feller when you're grown up, little man!'

'You think so?' asked her husband, peering doubtfully at the baby.

'I know so.' Her eyes shone. 'Take a look at the world today – all fightin' and grabbin' and greed. Nobody carin' to look after the weak and the innocent. What do we need if it isn't someone strong – someone above it all – to sort things out? Someone who couldn't be bullied or hurt. Someone who never got bone-weary of fighting the injustice. Maybe the Lord sent him to us for that very purpose – to clear up all the wickedness in the world.'

'Be a big responsibility, bringin' up that kind of a child,' said her husband.

'Yes,' she replied warmly.

They both gazed fondly at the baby, who, as though to punctuate the close of their conversation, gave a tiny, liquid sneeze.

A week later three frightened men stood in a hotel suite overlooking the main street of the state capital. One of them was the Governor; the other two were doctors. The building they occupied offered the best accommodation in town, and every room was normally booked weeks in advance. Today was different. With the exception of one other person, the three were alone in the hotel. Even the hotel staff were absent; they had gone to play their parts in the grotesque drama that was unfolding in the city streets.

A hysterical crowd was jamming Main Street, a swollen river of humanity that pushed, kicked and jostled its way along oblivious of all obstacles. Here and there a member of the mob struggled under the weight of an armful of personal belongings, but most of the crowd were solely concerned with flight. The Governor noticed a big, burly-looking man, smashing people out of his way with a pick-handle. The tip of the improvised club was already red and shiny.

Only an hour before there had been an orderly flow of traffic along the street. It was after the traffic jammed that the panic had set in, and now the crocodile of abandoned vehicles was merely a maddening obstacle to the mob. Car roofs had been crushed in by the weight of the bodies scrambling over them.

The Governor heard someone screaming in the distance. Glass broke. He turned away abruptly from the window.

'Where's Cade?' he asked his companions.

'Operating the switchboard in the lobby. He's trying to get through to the biology lab at the university. They were culturing samples there.'

They all turned as a young man ambled unhurriedly into the room.

'Well?' asked the Governor.

Cade did not reply at once. He trudged slowly to the window, staring out with an unreadable expression. From somewhere below they all heard the shrill, terrified voice of a woman, raised in inarticulate entreaty. It was abruptly terminated.

'Did you manage to get through?'

Cade shook his head.

'You mean they've abandoned the exchange?'

'Nope. It was just ringing. Nobody answered. I don't think anybody will, now.' He turned to face them all, his clenched fists dug deep into his pockets. 'I had one piece of luck, though. Got through to the Research Institute. They've been working on a batch of the stuff for two days. I didn't know.'

'Are they making any headway? How far have they got?'

'They've given up.'

The others gaped at him, too stunned to speak.

'They already knew that it was as immune to antibodies as a heap of iron filings, and they've spent the past forty-eight hours dosing it with penicillin and the newer antibiotics.'

'And . . . ?'

'No effect.' He inhaled shudderingly. 'And today – maybe for laughs, or maybe because they're going a little crazy – they dumped a culture into boiling sulphuric acid.' He opened and spread his hands in a gesture of surrender. 'The little S.O.B.'s just keep multiplying. Therefore, the team have decided that they are totally invulnerable, and therefore, the team have gone home to their families. I caught the last guy as he was on his way out. I wish to God we had time left to do the same.'

There was a long silence.

'How?' asked the Governor eventually. 'How is it possible?'

'Not that it matters any more, but I do have a theory. Most of the bacteria in the world, we can deal with. At least, our bodies can. That's because the germs – even the worst of them – are distant relatives of ours. We've grown up together over millions of years. Our antibodies know what makes them tick, and how to take them apart. Now this strain is completely different – so different that the only possible explanation for its existence is that—'

Suddenly, the crowd noise – to which they had all grown oblivious – changed horrifyingly in timbre. The gruff roaring of angry, crowded people was giving way to a piercing orchestration of terrified shrieks.

The four men rushed to the windows.

'Jesus!' Cade exclaimed. 'Look there! Down the street!'

For a moment it seemed as though the rear of the crowd had vanished; then, as more and more bodies fell to the ground, the horror revealed itself.

It was as though some unseen, poisonous liquid were flowing silently along the street. Beneath the hotel windows, the mob still screamed and fought; but only a little way behind, gaining ground inexorably, came death.

Rank by rank, people were dropping to the ground. A tough-looking man, evidently drunk, stood atop a battered delivery truck, thickly bawling what sounded like religious slogans. Suddenly his tirade faltered. He swayed unsteadily, his eyes sightless; and then there was a crash, and his lifeless body was sliding from the hood of the truck to join the tangle of corpses which now sprawled from one side of the road to the other.

Cade watched as a young woman fought to untwine

her dead child's arms from around her knees; in the midst of her struggle, she sank to the ground, her body covering the small one in a horrid parody of protectiveness.

'My God, this is horrible,' exclaimed the Governor. 'Maybe if we stay in here for a few days – there'll be food and drink downstairs—'

Cade interrupted him impatiently. 'Why? Do you think there's any escape from *that*?' He angrily indicated the windows, and what lay beyond them. 'It spreads through the air itself. It's here, now, among us. Probably incubating in our bloodstreams already.' His voice had an odd, slurred sound. One of the doctors took a pace back.

There was a horrid pause. Cade rocked on his heels. An unhealthy flush had mounted to his cheeks, and he peered at his companions narrowly, as though straining to see through thickening darkness.

'I must have brought it up from the lobby with me,' he said.

He looked around at them all, smiling in a kind of feverish wonderment; and then he toppled forward, and died at their feet.

A little while later there was no movement of any kind anywhere along Main Street except for the fluttering of wind-stirred summer clothing. For a time it was still possible to hear distant cries and confusions carried on the intermittent breeze from remote, still-living sections of the city; but these grew fainter and more infrequent, until at last there was no sound anywhere at all.

It was almost a fortnight before the last earthly life was extinguished. It took that long for the contagion, carried by all living things and by the winds and waters themselves, to envelop the planet completely. The final creatures to die were the luminous fishes of the deep ocean trenches. Then, for the first time since the emergence of life on dry land, a great silence reigned over the whole earth.

Or almost the whole earth. For somewhere in the vast stillness of North America, a child was crying inconsolably.

Man of Steel, *Woman of Kleenex*

by Larry Niven

He's faster than a speeding bullet. He's more powerful than a locomotive. He's able to leap tall buildings at a single bound. Why can't he get a girl?

At the ripe old age of forty,* Kal-El (alias Superman, alias Clark Kent) is still unmarried. Almost certainly he is still a virgin. This is a serious matter. The species itself is in danger!

An unwed Superman is a mobile Superman. Thus it has been alleged that those who chronicle the Man of Steel's adventures are responsible for his condition. But the cartoonists are not to blame.

Nor is Superman handicapped by psychological problems.

Granted that the poor oaf is not entirely sane. How could he be? He is an orphan, a refugee, and an alien. His homeland no longer exists in any form, save for gigatons upon gigatons of dangerous, prettily coloured rocks.

As a child and young adult, Kal-El must have been hard put to find an adequate father-figure. What human could control his antisocial behaviour? What human would dare try to punish him? His actual, highly social behaviour during this period indicates an inhuman self-restraint.

What wonder if Superman drifted gradually into schizophrenia? Torn between his human and kryptonian identities, he chose to be both, keeping his split personalities rigidly separate. A pyschotic desperation is evident in his defence of his 'secret identity'.

* Superman first appeared in *Action Comics*, June 1938.

But Superman's sex problems are strictly physiological, and quite real.

The purpose of this article is to point out some medical drawbacks to being a kryptonian among human beings, and to suggest possible solutions. The kryptonian humanoid must not be allowed to go the way of the pterodactyl and the passenger pigeon.

I

What turns on a kryptonian?

Superman is an alien, an extraterrestrial. His humanoid frame is doubtless the result of parallel evolution, as the marsupials of Australia resemble their mammalian counterparts. A specific niche in the ecology calls for a certain shape, a certain size, certain capabilities, certain eating habits.

Be not deceived by appearances. Superman is no relative to homo sapiens.

What arouses Kal-El's mating urge? Did kryptonian women carry some subtle mating cue at appropriate times of the year? Whatever it is, Lois Lane probably doesn't have it. We may speculate that she smells wrong, less like a kryptonian woman than like a terrestrial monkey. A mating between Superman and Lois Lane would feel like sodomy – and would be, of course, by church and common law.

II

Assume a mating between Superman and a human woman, designated LL for convenience.

Either Superman has gone completely schizo and believes himself to be Clark Kent; or he knows what he's doing, but no longer gives a damn. Forty years is a long time. For Superman it has been even longer. He has X-ray vision; he knows just what he's missing.*

The problem is this. Electroencephalograms taken of men and women during sexual intercourse show that orgasm resembles 'a kind of pleasurable epileptic attack'. One loses control over one's muscles.

Superman has been known to leave his fingerprints in steel and in hardened concrete, accidentally. What would he do to the woman in his arms during what amounts to an epileptic fit?

III

Consider the driving urge between a man and a woman, the monomaniacal urge to achieve greater and greater penetration. Remember also that we are dealing with kryptonian muscles.

Superman would literally crush LL's body in his arms, while simultaneously ripping her open from crotch to sternum, gutting her like a trout.

IV

Lastly, he'd blow off the top of her head.

Ejaculation of semen is entirely involuntary in the human male, and in all other forms of terrestrial life. It would be unreasonable to assume otherwise for a kryptonian. But with kryptonian muscles behind it,

* One should not think of Superman as a Peeping Tom. A biological ability must be used. As a child Superman may never have known that things had surfaces, until he learned to suppress his X-ray vision.

If millions of people tend shamelessly to wear clothing with no lead in the weave, that is hardly Superman's fault.

Kal-El's semen would emerge with the muzzle velocity of a machine gun bullet.*

In view of the foregoing, normal sex is impossible between LL and Superman.

Artificial insemination may give us better results.

V

First we must collect the semen. The globules will emerge at transsonic speeds. Superman must first ejaculate, then fly frantically after the stuff to catch it in a test tube. We assume that he is on the Moon, both for privacy and to prevent the semen from exploding into vapour on hitting air at such speeds.

He can catch the semen, of course, before it evaporates in vacuum. He's faster than a speeding bullet.

But can he keep it?

All known forms of kryptonian life have superpowers. The same must hold true of living kryptonian sperm. We may reasonably assume that kryptonian sperm are vulnerable only to starvation and to green kryptonite; that they can travel with equal ease through water, air, vacuum, glass, brick, boiling steel, solid steel, liquid helium or the core of a star; and that they are capable of translight velocities.

What kind of a test tube will hold such beasties?

Kryptonian sperm and their unusual powers will give us further trouble. For the moment we will assume (because we must) that they tend to stay in the seminal fluid, which tends to stay in a simple glass tube. Thus Superman and LL can perform artificial insemination.

At least there will be another generation of kryptonians.

Or will there?

* One can imagine that the Kent home in Smallville was riddled with holes during Superboy's puberty. And why did Lana Lang never notice *that*?

VI

A ripened but unfertilized egg leaves LL's ovary, begins its voyage down her Fallopian tube.

Some time later, tens of millions of sperm, released from a test tube, begin their own voyage up LL's Fallopian tube.

The magic moment approaches . . .

Can human breed with Kryptonian? Do we even use the same genetic code? On the face of it, LL could more easily breed with an ear of corn than with Kal-El. But coincidence does happen. If the genes match . . .

One sperm arrives before the others. It penetrates the egg, forms a lump on its surface. The cell wall now thickens to prevent other sperm from entering. Within the now-fertilized egg, changes take place . . .

And ten million kryptonian sperm arrive slightly late.

Were they human sperm, they would be out of luck. But these tiny blind things are more powerful than a locomotive. A thickened cell wall won't stop them. They will *all* enter the egg, obliterating it entirely in an orgy of microscopic gang rape. So much for artificial insemination.

But LL's problems are just beginning.

VII

Within her body there are still tens of millions of frustrated kryptonian sperm. The single egg is now too diffuse to be a target. The sperm scatter.

They scatter without regard to what is in their path. They leave curved channels, microscopically small. Presently all will have found their way to the open air.

That leaves LL with several million microscopic perforations all leading deep into her abdomen. Most of the channels will intersect one or more loops of intestine.

Peritonitis is inevitable. LL becomes desperately ill.

Meanwhile, tens of millions of sperm swarm in the air over Metropolis.

VIII

This is more serious than it looks.

Consider: these sperm are virtually indestructible. Within days or weeks they will die for lack of nourishment. Meanwhile they cannot be affected by heat, cold, vacuum, toxins, or anything short of green kryptonite.* There they are, miniscule but dangerous; for each has supernormal powers.

Metropolis is shaken by tiny sonic booms. Wormholes, charred by meteoric heat, sprout magically in all kinds of things: plate glass, masonry, antique ceramics, electric mixers, wood, household pets, and citizens. Some of the sperm will crack lightspeed. The Metropolis night comes alive with a network of narrow, eerie blue lines of Cherenkov radiation.

And women whom Superman has never met find themselves in a delicate condition.

Consider: LL won't get pregnant because there were too many of the blind mindless beasts. But whenever one sperm approaches an unfertilized human egg in its panic flight, it will attack.

How close is close enough? A few centimetres? Are sperm attracted by chemical cues? It seems likely. Metropolis had a population of millions; and a kryptonian sperm could travel a long and crooked path, billions of miles, before it gives up and dies.

Several thousand blessed events seem not unlikely.†

Several thousand lawsuits would follow. Not that

* And other forms of kryptonite. For instance, there are chunks of red kryptonite that make giants of kryptonians. Imagine ten million earthworm-sized spermatozoa swarming over a Metropolis beach, diving to fertilize the beach balls . . . but I digress.

† If the pubescent Superboy plays with himself, we have the same problem over Smallville.

Superman can't afford to pay. There's a trick where you squeeze a lump of coal into its allotropic diamond form . . .

IX

The above analysis gives us part of the answer. In our experiment in artificial insemination, we must use a single sperm. This presents no difficulty. Superman may use his microscopic vision and a pair of tiny tweezers to pluck a sperm from the swarm.

X

In its eagerness the single sperm may crash through LL's abdomen at transsonic speeds, wreaking havoc. Is there any way to slow it down?

There is. We can expose it to gold kryptonite.

Gold kryptonite, we remember, robs a kryptonian of all of his supernormal powers, permanently. Were we to expose Superman himself to gold kryptonite, we would solve all his sex problems, but he would be Clark Kent forever. We may regard this solution as somewhat drastic.

But we can expose the test tube of seminal fluid to gold kryptonite, then use standard techniques for artificial insemination.

By any of these methods we can get LL pregnant, without killing her. Are we out of the woods yet?

XI

Though exposed to gold kryptonite, the sperm still carries kryptonian genes. If these are recessive, then LL carries a developing human foetus. There will be no more Supermen; but at least we need not worry about the mother's health.

But if some or all of the kryptonian genes are dominant . . .

Can the infant use his X-ray vision before birth? After all, with such a power he can probably see through his own closed eyelids. That would leave LL sterile. If the kid starts using heat vision, things get even worse.

But when he starts to kick, it's all over. He will kick his way out into the open air, killing himself and his mother.

XII

Is there a solution?

There are several. Each has drawbacks.

We can make LL wear a kryptonite* belt around her waist. But too little kryptonite may allow the child to damage her, while too much may damage or kill the child. Intermediate amounts may do both! And there is no safe way to experiment.

A better solution is to find a host-mother.

We have not yet considered the existence of Supergirl.† She could carry the child without harm. But Supergirl has a secret identity, and her secret identity is no more married than Supergirl herself. If she turned up pregnant, she would probably be thrown out of school.

A better solution may be to implant the growing foetus in Superman himself. There are places in a man's

* For our purposes, all forms of kryptonite are available in unlimited quantities. It has been estimated, from the startling tonnage of kryptonite fallen to Earth since the explosion of krypton, that the planet must have outweighed our entire solar system. Doubtless the 'planet' Krypton was a cooling black dwarf star, one of a binary pair, the other member being a red giant.

† She can't mate with Superman because she's his first cousin. And only a cad would suggest differently.

abdomen where a foetus could draw adequate nourishment, growing as a parasite, and where it would not cause undue harm to surrounding organs. Presumably Clark Kent can take a leave of absence more easily than Supergirl's schoolgirl alter ego.

When the time comes, the child would be removed by Caesarian section. It would have to be removed early, but there would be no problem with incubators as long as it was fed. I leave the problem of cutting through Superman's invulnerable skin, as an exercise for the alert reader.

The mind boggles at the image of a pregnant Superman cruising the skies of Metropolis. Batman would refuse to be seen with him; strange new jokes would circulate the prisons . . . and the race of Krypton would be safe at last.